Follow the Script

Follow the Script

A Novella

Stacy Wright

Follow the Script

Book design by Maureen Cutajar
www.gopublished.com

ISBN: 979-8469761273

To my wonderful grandchildren,

you are my inspiration, and my reward in life.

ACKNOWLEDGEMENTS

As with most everything I manage to accomplish these days, I have to thank my wife Ann. She's my biggest supporter, and the best proof reader I've ever known. I have to mention my son Brandon. What he does each day inspires me, and his encouragement pushed me forward with this writing project. My other son John, your editing skills simply cannot go unmentioned sir, thank you. I cannot forget my oldest granddaughter Sedona, her honest critique of an original draft helped to shape what I believe to be a better written story.

I want to thank Robin Vuchnich of My Custom Book Cover for the graphic design creation. Also, thanks to Maureen Cutajar of Go Published for the interior formatting. Thank you both for not only your services, but your cheerful guidance through the process.

⸨ Prologue ⸩

Southern Vista Police Precinct,
Saguaro, Arizona, April 2020

SAGUARO, ARIZONA, SMACK IN the middle of the state, a hot desert landscape, that in the last century was turned into farmland, but more recently, transformed into urban sprawl and suburban escapes. The largest city in Arizona, it serves as the location of the State Capitol and the Seat of Hohokam County. In Arizona, Saguaro is where big decisions are made, both good and bad. The Southern Vista Police Precinct has arguably been known as the area of the city where crime has most historically flourished, In recent years, that could no longer be said as the criminals migrated north, west and east, essentially spreading their toxic wealth over what were once considered to be safe, wholesome neighborhoods; Saguaro is a city happy to share its pain amongst all its residents. Down in South Saguaro, things aren't really that different now than the rest of the city. There's still crime, but the days of gang gunfights in the streets are pretty much over and in fact, new homes are being built as are efforts to rebuild previously abandoned tract home subdivisions.

Newly promoted to Sergeant Kevin Galway was still in training. He passed the test months earlier, but in the Saguaro police department, a dangerously understaffed organization mired down with political poison, things move very slowly. Galway was told he will soon be assigned a patrol squad in a yet defined precinct and in the meantime, he could pretty much do whatever he wanted in order to 'better prepare himself' for his next leadership assignment. Translation; "Drive around on an open channel, listening for any interesting calls in the city and go see what's happening." Easy work for now and an assignment his wife of 2 years loves. She would be happy if he never left the precinct house, she hates that he's a cop, scared to death he's going to be killed on the job. Galway even being an officer is odd. As a kid he never thought about being a cop at all, his father wanted him to become a plumber like his cousins in Brockton Massachusetts, they made good money. In fact, that was Kevin's plan until a friend from high school was shot and killed while standing in line at a small family grocery store as an armed robbery erupted; plumbing no longer interested him, but taking criminals out did. Sgt. Kevin Galway loves his new wife, but he can't leave the street if criminals are out there, it's what he does and he refuses to change. He hears a dispatched call over the air for his old Southern Vista Precinct that suddenly, changes everything for him; his mind, his mood and his soul, this isn't good.

As the last rays of sunlight illuminate the south valley neighborhood, Galway spots a half dozen police vehicles and a growing crowd of spectators, gawking and pointing at the particular house the cops are busy with. Walking through an open side gate leading to the backyard, he sees a circle of young, uniformed officers all pointing, discussing and even laughing, when he's spotted by the senior officer on the scene.

"Hey Sarge, what brings you to the hood, why aren't you with your new squad, leading them all to careers of crime fighting glory?" This was an older cop Galway had worked with for years in the Southern Precinct, one of many who elect to rise no higher than patrol officer status, something the civilian working community would not easily understand; many cops don't want the added responsibility and political games that come with leadership positions.

"Hey you guys. Take a look at one of the original Horsemen, a Southern Vista legend!" the smiling old cop announces loudly to his uniformed audience. The gaggle of young, wary cops simply stare, a couple that could easily still be in High School by the looks of them.

Galway answers his old squad mate; "Come on Vince, stop that shit, crime fighting glory? Yeah right, more like keep your head down and that 20-year pension will be here in what will easily seem like 50!" Some chuckles and the young cops go back to interviewing a young Hispanic man and an equally young pregnant woman, who was trying to keep a little girl of about 2 from bolting toward the side gate.

"Actually Vince, I'm still waiting to pick up a squad somewhere and for now I'm technically in training, just riding the radio, picking up calls I might be able to assist with. The selection process sucks, it takes forever and I'm ready to get on with it'" says Galway truthfully about the delays, but then continues, with a less genuine statement and question; "There ain't shit going on right now and this call sounded interesting, so what do you got exactly?"

The old patrol cop explains the situation; "See the young Mexican kid over there, his wife and the toddler? Christ she'll have six more before she's 30, but anyway, this is one of the refurbished houses the City subsidized trying to bring the area back to life, this couple bought in. The kid seems cool enough; he works for the City in Parks and Recreation. He was out to dig a hole for that tree over there before it got dark...I'm guessing the tree came from City Parks landscape stock and not Home Depot if you get my drift. Anyway he found a little surprise, come take a look!"

On the ground next to a dirty military canvas duffle bag was a pile of rusted AK-47 style rifles, a few handguns and what looked to be an UZI. The young cops were taking pictures with their phones. Later, crime scene techs will be taking quality photographs of the scene and the guns, which will be bagged and inspected for serial numbers and possible fingerprints. Based on the surface rust visible on the firearms, finding viable fingerprints isn't likely.

"Sarge remember back in the day, when this area was like the Wild fucking West, more drop houses here than real families? I figure some shit head got scared, maybe had word they'd be raided and buried their stash. It's too bad though, some of those shooters might have been keepers. Not now though, that's a worthless pile of rusted crap right there, we'll let the techs deal with it."

Galway agreed with the assessment, shook Vince's hand and after a mutual exchange of not letting the shitheads ever win, he headed to his marked Tahoe and drove north, getting as far away from the Southern Vista precinct as fast as he could drive, regretting now having ever heard the damn radio call. Pulling out his cell phone he hits a contact and waits, the call is answered; "Yeah hey, it's me, look, we got a problem."

{ CHAPTER 1 }

Downtown Saguaro, four months later

IT IS ONLY 8AM and already hot in Saguaro, Arizona. The desert lands of Arizona have two seasons: 6 months of blazing hot summer and 6 months of a not so blazing hot winter. It's not all that much cooler inside the old Del Vista West Hotel where Ben Morris currently calls home. For many years, in its heyday, the Del Vista West was the tallest building west of the mighty Mississippi River. The days of hosting presidents and Hollywood movie stars have long since passed. The building today is viewed by the taxpayers of the city to be a madhouse, something to be avoided, a black eye to society. Today it functions as a government subsidized housing facility for recovering drug addicts, homeless persons of all sorts, struggling military veterans and sadly in the mix, are many mentally challenged persons that have no real places to be treated; this being at least a temporary place to exist in a mostly cruel life. The housing environment also serves another purpose, that of being a quasi-halfway house for recently released convicts.

That is where Ben Morris fits into the mosaic of the residents; having served a 6-month sentence in the Hohokam County jail for illegal drug crimes, he qualified for these quarters based on his successful completion of a drug rehabilitation course during his time behind bars. He is definitely not happy with his surroundings, but it clearly beats the hell out of the county jail, where he lost 15 pounds from an already trim body. His time behind bars would have been miserable for anyone, but for a man with movie star good looks, he was a target the minute he was found guilty in court. He benefitted from a bit of local notoriety and the jail staff helped to ensure he was not allowed to 'enjoy' the normal unsavory treatment inside the jail, something Ben was and is very thankful for. That same notoriety, now in his current situation is paying zero dividends. He is a lost man wandering in a hard, uncaring world, not what he was once used to. Those halcyon days seem like a million years ago, the right here and now is what has his attention as he needs to secure a job quickly. A major requirement, within his probation release agreement, is to find employment and so far he has struck out badly.

It's not like Ben did not try to get back to what he knows, but after his embarrassing arrest and conviction, even those in the industry, those he thought to be friends, refused his calls. A far cry from the bright future and dreams he had as a kid in college, earning a degree in journalism. He always went to good schools and after college, almost immediately found employment in the print news business, starting as a reporter, but moving up quickly as an investigative reporter and eventually branched into the television media market. He was once the talk of the town, reporting for Channel 14, a very popular, unaffiliated television station. The station had achieved several prestigious reporting awards over the years, Ben being directly responsible for more than one of the impressive achievements.

Only one low level producer actually agreed to talk to him and even then was reluctant, afraid it would be discovered and risked losing his job. That's how toxic Ben Morris had become. It wasn't just the bad publicity, but the concern that his previous award-winning investigations might now be seen as tainted. There was the real concern that lawsuits spawning from previously exposed and defamed individuals, targets of the station's investigations, many with heavy political weight and money, the fear was very possible some of these individuals would seek financial revenge if they sensed an opportunity. For Channel 14, they hoped the name of Ben Morris would be forever forgotten. The media business, although technically competitors, they stick together in certain times and this was one of those times. For now, Ben's only real job skill and profession was at a dead end; say hello to unskilled labor opportunities, if he could find one. Ben Morris does not have much experience with menial, low skilled labor employment, but he desperately needs to find some sort of work. His very attentive Probation Officer, Julio Chavez, painfully reminds him of this each week.

Unfortunately for Ben, it seems that PO Julio Chavez has developed a deep dislike for case number "PO1958". Before Ben was a number to Chavez, he was the news reporter media darling, his perfect teeth and 'pretty boy' good looks, no doubt making a fortune, driving a Mercedes and likely sleeping with the perfect "Barbie Doll" female anchors on the news desk and Chavez resented every bit of it, real or imagined. In Julio Chavez's world, he felt he was being forced to put up with worthless scum, dishonest losers, who, in his opinion, should have never been released back into society. Why should a spoiled punk like Ben Morris catch all the breaks in life, while he was stuck in the toilet, swirling around with the floating turds of society? At least Ben is aware of Chavez's contempt.

Thankfully Ben does not have to check in with Julio Chavez for another 3 days, maybe today something will open up in the 'Art' district for a janitor or table cleaner in the many, many coffee bistros, folk art and 'New Age' businesses. That's the closest he's come to having someone at least listen to his plight and need for help, best to try it again and it's only a few blocks to walk, which in the already blazing heat is probably the only blessing Ben can find in his miserable life at the moment.

"Nope, no, nothing today, try next week or when it cools off", "It's the hot season, hey good luck my brother in life, bless your soul…", the typical responses Ben has become accustomed to, but at least here in the Art District they're kind in their rejection responses, unlike the mechanic shops, fast food/ethnic family food joints and seemingly every other sort of business. Ben is becoming accustomed to the pain of rejection, but it's still best to receive it in somewhat, smaller and friendlier doses as opposed to "GET OUT AND DON'T ASK AGAIN!" Time for one more stop before the long walk to the government buildings all in and around the downtown area in the heart of Saguaro, where he will stand in line at the unemployment and food stamp (now called EBT) offices. Figuring he'll spend most of the remaining day seeking assistance, he hopes above all that the lines don't trail out too far into the blazing heat and he can at least stand inside the building. Time to put on his best smile and hope this time it scores him a job, any job.

"Bathsheba's Rainbow Bistro", is the destination of his next and likely latest rejection. To his surprise, owner Bathsheba (real name Shelley Conner) herself is sweeping the sidewalk in front of her bistro. At 5' 6", 200 pounds, swarthy, tattooed, enough visible body piercings to add even more weight to her already substantial frame, she stops sweeping and eyes Ben Morris with her normal and clearly visual fierce stare. "Hey pretty boy, I was hoping you'd come by, I might have something for you by way of work, you interested?"

Stunned, Ben blurts out, "Yes, anything you have, I really, really need it!"

"Slow your fucking roll dude, I'm not looking to take down Amazon with a new business and a shit load of employees, I need someone that can serve coffee and clean up paper cups at the goddamn park. Can you handle it or are you too delicate for that?" she asks harshly.

"Oh no, no, no, I was just surprised and, oh and thankful, I just wasn't expecting to hear this, that's all....YES, I can do all of that, YES!" Ben says, clearly unprepared for this news.

"Well take a breath before you get the vapors, you don't even know what I might pay you and what exactly it is you will really do and WON'T do. You still interested?" the fierce eyed Bathsheba/Shelley asks.

"Oh yes ma'am, I'm just so thankful, please, thank you, I really need this job!" says an eager Ben.

Bathsheba eyes him hard and says, "Call me ma'am ever again and I'll give your old TV station the biggest story they ever reported as a man literally has his head stuck up his own ass, we good on that?"

Ben stumbles out with an embarrassing, "Yes Ma'…err I mean Ms. Bathsheba or boss?"

Still assessing him, Bathsheba finally says, "On every Saturday at "Vance Park", we set up like all the freaks in this area to sell shit. I need help because one of my girls decided she wasn't as dedicated to 'hole' as much as she was to 'pole', the stupid little bitch, but no matter, I need help, you still in?"

"Oh yes, Ma…. Bathsheba, I'm definitely in and I won't let you down, I can't thank you enough!" a still in shock Ben says.

"Geezus, stop sucking up you whiny little prick, I know who you are and as worthless as you might be, I need your pretty face to draw in the business, primarily chicks, which you'll dutifully point my way, got it?", the glaring Bathsheba reveals.

Stunned, Ben responds with; "Oh sure, I clearly get it, I'm totally good with that and I'll make sure any hot ladies are sent your way!"

"That quick huh, what happened? Did those boys in the county change your mind about liking pretty girls? It wouldn't be the first time you know?" Bathsheba smirks, her first show of emotion other than that of barely restrained fury.

Ignoring the insult, Ben immediately says, "I'm in, when exactly do I have to be there and where in the park, plus what will I be paid?"

Surprisingly, Bathsheba responds with, "Good, I need the help and I liked some of the work you did on TV, but boy, you sure let your dick and your nose lead you off track. Well, you wouldn't be the first. Saturday morning at the park, if I'm not selling coffee by 7AM I might as well not even waste my fucking time. You be there at 5AM, Jesus will be there with a trailer and tell you what to do…I hope you can speak Español, anyway, we run to 10PM, and don't bitch about labor laws, this is a circus show, freaks like you don't set the rules, I do. So, you still interested?"

"I'm interested, but you didn't say what I'd be paid, is it hourly or what?" a cautious sounding Ben asks, thinking already he's made a mistake.

"Hourly? What the fuck boy, I'm guessing you'll want to know about the 401K Plan next? Sweet cheeks, you need to wake up from your dream world, this is reality now. You'll get paid $50 bucks cash off the books if you do the hours and Jesus says you were useful. Does that work for you or do you need to consult with your talent agent and financial planner?" an indignant Bathsheba asks.

Shamed, Ben meekly responds, "No Ma…I mean Bathsheba, that's very fair and I promise I won't let you down. I can speak some Spanish, but it's more functional by necessity than fluent. A question though, can I list you as an employer even though I'm not going to be getting a paycheck? I really need to show I'm finding employment?"

In an immediate and staunch manner, Bathsheba responds with; "Sure, I guess I'd know why that might be important, but you actually have to earn that $50 bucks first sonny. I think I might eventually want to even try liking you, but not enough to lie for you. You work Saturday and earn it first, then yeah, I'm good with it."

"Okay, thank you again Bathsheba, I won't let you down!" Ben sincerely says to her, but quietly knows he has an issue with this timing.

"One other thing, unless customers are within earshot, call me Shelley. Bathsheba is only the name for the store to draw in customers…Jesus has issues with both, but 'Chelley' is closer than whatever the hell it is he does with Bathsheba." This being the response from Ben Morris's new employer now to be addressed as Shelley, professionally known as Bathsheba.

Success! Ben Morris has found a job, albeit a small, cash paying event with zero known future, but it's paying $50 dollars. $50 dollars would have been a conservative dinner tip 2 years previously, but it's the only promise of earned money since his life ran off the edge of the Grand Canyon at high speed. Saturday is only 5 days away and he'll be ready. The problem is he has to meet with his probation officer in 3 days. Julio Chavez will certainly not be impressed or likely even to believe Ben's announcement of a 'cash only' paying event. Life always seemed so easy for Ben Morris, every domino falling perfectly into place. Now however, instead of dominos with comfortable number dots, he only sees similar sized tiles marked with nothing but chaos.

{ CHAPTER 2 }

Mid-city revival district,
Saguaro, Arizona, April 2020

Off-duty Saguaro police officer Marcus Johnson, having just received a troubling call from an old squad mate, now known as Sergeant Kevin Galway, really isn't surprised by the news. Deep down he has been expecting it for years, but remained hopeful it would never come. In fact, he and Galway have not actually spoken in years, in person or by phone, there was no reason to. Galway stayed back in the old precinct, eventually made the promotion in grade and just recently moved north in the city to take on a squad of his own. Johnson, on the other hand, didn't seek the limelight after leaving the south precinct nearly 20 years earlier. He worked, initially as a patrol officer in more sedate city locations, then for a time at the airport, and over the last two years, as a school resource officer at a K-8 school in the mid-city area of Saguaro. With 20 years under his belt, he planned to coast peacefully a few more years 'on the job' to pad his pension numbers, which suited him just fine. Unfortunately, his plan was not likely to happen now. This news from Galway wasn't going to keep. It would break in a bad way.

Marcus questions why he decided to leave Atlanta Georgia where he was born and raised. A cousin that played collegiate football in central Arizona at the time, made it sound like a warm paradise, a great place where young black men could thrive and forget the prevalent racial discrimination, which seemed impossible to escape from in the deep south. "Not the case in Arizona", his cousin said, "None of that racist shit exists here in Arizona Cuz". Which in all fairness to his cousin, who enjoyed a full football scholarship, was a star on the team and likely headed to the NFL, his opinion was probably accurate based on his unique perspective. For everyone else though, opinions vary drastically on the subject.

Marcus quickly came to realize that no place is completely without discrimination, and being a black man, his experience in Arizona was in fact better, when it came to how blacks and whites relate, no question about it. Living in Atlanta, he never would have considered that 'brown' people would discriminate against blacks and Arizona has many brown skinned people. The move was an eye-opener for him in many ways, but nothing like he would have ever imagined when seen through the eyes of a police officer, which is how he views the world. Atlanta was a dead-end for him in late 1998. His steady, low paying job at a bottling company was not what he thought of as a career. Being able to live at his mother's home allowed him enough money to have a car, enjoy life, and many women, none that he would ever introduce to his Mama. Marcus was looking for a change. After hearing his cousin's description of Arizona, he decided to pack what belongings he had into his car, say goodbye to a tearful Mama and head out to Saguaro Arizona, where he would find happiness and fulfill his dreams of success. Looking back, he had at least found Saguaro, Arizona.

The Saguaro area certainly had work opportunities for unskilled workers and apartment housing was cheap, which was a plus. However, none of the job opportunities offered anything by way of health benefits or retirement benefits. Marcus was savvy about these things, which his late father drilled into him. It was how his mother now lived comfortably in a paid-off home. His first job upon arriving in Saguaro was at a car dealership parking and washing cars. One day, he saw a billboard that the local Saguaro Police Department was looking for recruits, so he filled out an application. He was accepted, pending a positive physical, psychological profile and a passing score on a basic written test. May 1999 was the scheduled start date for the 4 month training academy.

As odd as it had been, Marcus found himself remarkably well suited for law enforcement, even without planning on being a cop. He had excelled in all phases of the very grueling training program, becoming more focused on a career in fighting crime, more so than caring about the provided benefits. During a late phase of the academy, an older cop came to address the remaining recruits; those that had not dropped out and were highly likely to graduate and move on to field training. Unlike their 'spit and polish' training officers, this cop had been different altogether; he had the literal vibe of being a warrior; fit looking, tall, hard and a look in his eye that had been difficult to meet.

His message had been blunt.

"Take a look at the people around you now because in less than a year, many will be gone, they certainly won't be wearing a badge. Many won't make it through field training even if you graduate this academy. Then even more will quit during the first few months after field training because it's too ugly…it's scary and it's FUCKING HARD! Take another look around you because chances are good that before you all enjoy cashing in your pension checks, many in this group will be killed flat out, that's the way it goes. A few more will fuck up and be fired for good cause because for them, deep down inside, they don't have the true integrity it takes to be a cop; they just fake it better than others."

The warrior continued, "Ah, but there's a few more here that can be referred to as 'bonus round' candidates."

"The bonus round is the one you rack into that sidearm sitting in your holster, just before you suck on the barrel and put a fucking bullet in your brain because it all becomes too much, none of which was covered in the recruiting brochure the department handed out to help get you here. It sucks, but at least they weren't pussies."The warrior paused.

"'The pussies', you ask? They're in here too if you look close enough, but initially they're hard to spot. They won't be able to hide for long though. You'll recognize them as being the ones that never seem to be able to respond to an assist call, always with an excuse. They will seek the easy way out. They will avoid action at all costs. They were never a true brother or sister in the badge, only in it for the benefits. If that's not bad enough, many will eventually move into command positions lording over you."

"The rest of you left standing? Well, you were likely 'tapped' on the shoulder suddenly by an invisible force pushing you to be a cop. Like when God taps a person to become a man of the cloth. Whatever tapped you though couldn't have been God, because the time will come where you'll believe there simply can't be a God of mercy, not with the horrors you'll see. If it was God that did tap you, he has one sick fucking sense of humor."

Hearing that speaker, Marcus Johnson had been certain that in 1999 God had tapped him on the shoulder. He had been destined to be a cop, a warrior. He would certainly never hide like the pussies in the speech. Marcus will soon find out that 'never' has an actual expiration date.

{ CHAPTER 3 }

Probation Headquarters,
Saguaro, Arizona, August 2020

About the time that the 'fallen from grace' journalist, Ben Morris, receives news that he might have scored a low paying, unsteady job opportunity, Morris' probation officer Julio Chavez was sitting at his small desk going over today's case load. None of what he sees pleases him. In fact, extraordinarily little about this 'career' pleases him; it was nothing close to what he had planned for his life. Chavez is a native to Saguaro, born in the west side, a mostly Latino area at a time before drugs and gang violence became the norm. Chavez never would have fallen in with that sort of criminal element; his strong family upbringing would not have allowed it. He had been a good student, playing Little League, Babe Ruth and High School baseball. He had hoped for a baseball scholarship at least to a Community College, but it never happened.

What did happen was his meeting with an Army recruiter and enlisting with the hopes of becoming a military policeman, like his uncle and baseball coach had done, 2 decades earlier. His Army career was on track with his plan to retire from the Army. Once the Army was behind him, he intended to return to Saguaro, Arizona with the idea of becoming a police officer, preferably with the State Police, long ago known as "The Highway Patrol". After 4 good years in the Army, he had married and reenlisted for another tour of duty. He liked his job and had been able to take college courses along the way. This was a career path he had felt was made in heaven just for him. By his sixth year in the Army, he now had a young son and his wife was expecting their second child. Then his perfect world seemed to have stepped into something like the Twilight Zone.

One day at the Army post headquarters, having just returned from a shoplifting call at the base commissary, where an Army brat had tried to lift a bag of chips and some candy bars, Chavez had been doing some paperwork and laughing with his team, when suddenly he had begun to sweat profusely. His heart had felt like it was going to beat itself out of his chest, he felt dizzy and the next thing he knew he had woken in the base hospital. The doctors had diagnosed him with a sudden onset heart murmur/arrhythmia, treatable through medications and the possibility of a pace maker, which had been good medical news. The bad news had been that he was no longer medically fit for the Army. In just over a month, he had been medically discharged under honorable conditions, a stunning turn of events for Chavez and his young family. He returned to Saguaro, Arizona, and with help from his extensive family, had found a temporary place to live. His medical condition had also prevented him from becoming a police officer, which was a real blow. If there was any upside, he was only one semester short of finishing a Bachelor's Degree. He had immediately enrolled in college and applied for minor jobs, checking in often with the VA doctors at the downtown hospital.

Between jobs that essentially were created for him by family members, Julio had drawn unemployment benefits when he qualified. It had taken him nearly a year before earning his degree and qualifying for better job opportunities. He now had a young son, an even younger daughter and a wife that had desperately tried to hide her fear and deep concern about their family's future.

With a college degree in hand, Chavez applied for anything and everything that might provide benefits and reasonable pay. During a job fair he had attended, he had been drawn toward the law enforcement recruiting displays, a no-go zone in his mind, when he noticed the final table had a display and lonely recruiter looking for anyone interested in becoming a probations officer. Chavez was interested because it had seemed sort of like law enforcement, but from a different perspective. He told the recruiter straight out about his medical situation and had been assured that it would not exclude him from applying, nor prevent him from attending the probations officer academy. Wow! It had sounded great and he had filled out an application right then and there. Apparently there had rarely been a long line at the probation officer recruiting table according to the excited young man with the brochures and papers, but it had to beat working with his uncle's landscaping/roofing tear-off crew, which can be brutal in nearly year-round Arizona heat.

To his surprise, he was accepted and graduated top of his academy class. He was now employed by the County of Hohokam, Arizona. It came with a very modest salary and although the benefits were good, the job itself sucked. Even as an Army MP, the whole idea had been to catch criminals so they could face justice. He had never considered what happened after that. Now dealing with supposedly (questionably in his mind) reformed criminals, he struggled to assist them with rejoining society. He had tried to follow the mantra he must have heard 15 thousand times in the academy; to always assist your clients in a productive and positive way. Julio Chavez had developed a personal mantra that he never shared, but it was far from productive or positive.

Deep down Julio Chavez still wanted to be the guy that put the shitheads in jail, not the one that helped them back out of custody. The fact was, he had a wife and two kids to support, with mounting bills to pay. This was the hand he'd been dealt in the sad game of life poker. He wasn't happy about it, but he had little choice except to play his cards. In the meantime, God help any of his 'clients' that rubbed him the wrong way, sending them back behind bars wouldn't do anything except produce a wide internal smile.

{ CHAPTER 4 }

3rd Shift, Midtown Precinct, Saguaro, Arizona

Sergeant Kevin Galway is on patrol and riding alone on a brutally hot summer night in the Midtown Precinct. Galway now has a squad of his own and he likes his team. He only wants the best for them; keeping them all safe is his top priority. As is typical for a Sergeant, he's riding solo while some squad members double-up as criminal activities dictate. Still, a few others patrol alone depending on their seniority and experience. Galway keeps track of what's happening in the area by monitoring radio traffic, always knowing where his units are being deployed. They all have cell phones to communicate with as well, it's as good as they can hope for, but the reality is they need more officers so every unit would have 2 cops, it's that dangerous on the street. Everything seems to be going well tonight, it's now midnight, which puts temps right around 100 degrees; the pavement and concrete jungle simply doesn't cool at night like it did 50 years earlier, all thanks to urban sprawl, or what politicians call progress.

When it's hot during the day, the shit heads don't come out, they find air conditioning or even shade will do, but after the sun goes down, even if it's still hot outside, the sun isn't beating down so hard the asphalt softens, they venture out for trouble. This is why 3rd shift is different and explosively active at times. From about 11PM until 2AM, except for bar fights and DUI stops (which they hate) there's a lull, but like clockwork, around 3AM cars start getting stolen, businesses are getting broken into, fires randomly start, gunfire erupts, it's crazy time. This is the exact lull Kevin Galway has been waiting for tonight due to a personal task he's assigned himself.

The fact is, over the past month Galway has been multi-tasking; a Patrol Sergeant running a squad of crime fighters, yet also as a private detective of sorts for his own purposes all while on the clock, but not for much longer. Galway has secretly been working a complicated case on his own, the department doesn't know, in fact no one else knows about it. The case he's been working on involves a suicide made to look like a homicide to police officers. It was well thought out; happening in an area of the city known to have security cameras, but with one blind spot few people are aware of. On top of that, it's in a high crime area where homicides and assaults occur often. Police would have little reason to suspect suicide in an area like this. Why would so much detailed planning be needed for such a staged event? Money would be a likely motive. Money is almost always the motive. Suicide voids most life insurance policies, as well as any company benefits due the surviving spouses. This was clearly the motive as far as Galway was concerned, the 'victim' wanted to make the suicide look like a homicide so the insurance money would be paid out to the spouse. His sleuthing of the spouse indicated that she definitely needed the insurance and benefit pay-outs. Galway thought to himself that he could actually be a good detective if he wasn't a patrol Sergeant on the Saguaro Police Department, something he had dreamed of since he entered the police academy in 1999, so many years ago.

Tonight, Patrol Sergeant Galway would put his detective skills to the test to determine if he was right or wrong. Back in April, when he decided to drive down and check in on a squad responding to a dispatched radio call in his old south Saguaro precinct, a call that involved a young homeowner unearthing a pile of rusted guns, that minor event started something within Kevin Galway. That odd call for police service had prompted him to shift his priorities and mindset onto the case he has been secretly working so extensively on the last couple of months. Except for the phone call he made to a long-ago squad mate that night, while rapidly driving away from south Saguaro, no one, not his wife nor his parents knew how much the case disturbed him. He had at that point realized that this was something only he alone could tackle.

The problem with any complicated case, such as this, is that unless you have direct witness testimony or a confession from a suspect admitting to the event, results of a crime are often left to speculation and differences of opinion between police detectives and court juries. Kevin does not want that, he needs to make the case he's working on clear and irrefutable. He's a cop that demands and delivers results.

He hears a call over the radio, nothing serious, but he asks one of his senior patrol officers to meet him at a local gas/convenience store chain that caters to cops. During summer months, the store(s) not only allow officers to walk into the 'cold box', where beer and soft drinks are stored, but they encourage it so the cops can recover from the insane heat and by their presence, helps keep the shitheads away due to the frequent rotating cop visits. The two savvy street cops discuss the progress and general state of the newer members, how they're advancing or not taking to the harsh environment, etc. According to the senior officer, who is older than Sergeant Galway by 3 years, but who clearly has respect for his supervisor because he came to the realization long ago that he himself was unwilling to take on the BS of being in a position of leadership, especially now in what he sees to be a rapidly declining career field. His opinion of the young squad though is very positive. In fact he sees some real hard chargers on the team. This comes as music to Galway's ears. With only a few current radio calls for minor service in the queue, his team seemingly secure, the two veterans laugh about some inside shit only cops can relate to, then both drive off in different directions to continue the shift.

Kevin Galway has some important work to get to. Tonight he will prove that a suicide can be carefully staged to look like a homicide. The real problem Galway has had since that radio call from down in the Southern Vista Precinct about the buried cache of guns, is that his current case lacked one important thing: a victim. After tonight, there will finally be a victim to add to the case file. That victim will be the once proud Sergeant Kevin Galway himself. The big lie is finally over and he's actually relieved, which means there will only be one 'Horseman' left standing.

⁂ CHAPTER 5 ⁂

Job or Jail?

It was so damn hot and only 9AM, on top of that, Ben Morris hadn't slept a wink since he forced himself to lay down the night before on his crappy hotel/apartment/half-way house bed, which in his mind, was only a questionable upgrade from the previous steel cot with a permanently stained and threadbare cloth covering that he had enjoyed for 6 months in the county jail. Sleeping accommodations aside, that wasn't the reason for Ben Morris's lack of pleasant slumber, not even close. What really kept him up all night were his thoughts regarding the mandatory visit this morning with his very strict and intimidating Probation Officer, Mr. Julio Chavez. In Ben's mind, Chavez is worse than the jail guards he had encountered because they didn't seem to show blanket animosity toward the jail prisoners or what the progressive new Sheriff refers to now as jail 'occupants'. Whatever the term, if you were in jail, the guards knew they had a job to do and if you were following the rules, things were cool. That's not the way it is with Probation Officer Chavez, he seems to be angry with everything about Ben, well, at least that's the way it feels. Chavez might be different with others on probation, in fact Ben suspects so, he thinks Chavez has had an issue with him from the start and doesn't understand why. That's all out of his control. Right now, he just needs to stay focused this morning at the downtown Probation Headquarter offices. Ben intends to show enthusiasm for the upcoming job on Saturday working for "Bathsheba's Rainbow Bistro", make it known that this job has the potential for more hours of employment...it will be a tall task.

After signing in, Ben was eyeing the free coffee pot table in the corner, with powdered condiments, but apparently no staffer had filled the pot with water or brewed any coffee. From the looks of the crust inside the carafe, no one had done so in a good number of days or even weeks. Coffee not being an option, Ben looked around the Spartan room and counted 6 hard plastic chairs with rounded steel frames. The design ensured the chair legs could not be used as a weapon, exactly the kind used in the county jail and the out-of-site holding area for the county court rooms. Ben was not alone, there was a woman sitting nervously on one of the chairs, biting at seemingly non-existent nails. Her long straggly hair was a mix of blonde, gray and black streaks. She also had the unmistakable sign of a crystal meth user: "Meth Mouth". Crystal methamphetamine, or meth, will deliver an immediate high, like 'speed' from back in the 60's, or the high state of energy delivered from 'crack cocaine' in the late 80's and 90's. Not that speed or cocaine should be considered to be healthy or harmless, crystal meth is actually toxic to the human body. It's common for users to have sudden and manic energy bursts of such magnitude, they will sometimes remove all the furniture in their house or apartment, just to 'finally' get back there and clean where you always wanted to, but never did, and then, they would put it all back quicker than saying "methamphetamine!" That form of energy swoon can last for hours to days. With repeated use, users suddenly realize they are losing teeth, developing sores and lesions on their face and body. Any money that could be spent for a dentist is directed solely for the purchasing of more meth.

The woman in the waiting room had an ugly, flat, toothless, shrunken mouth, hence the term "Meth Mouth", as used on the streets and by law enforcement. This explained why she looked like an old, cackling, corn-cob pipe smoking, granny from the Appalachian Mountains circa 1850, or as Ben's imagination produced, the perfect Halloween witch. Ben Morris has never used crystal meth, speed or crack cocaine. Certainly not a prude or completely unfamiliar with illicit drugs, Ben has stylishly snorted powder cocaine and smoked exotic marijuana while drinking extremely expensive wines and spirits with the 'movers and shakers' of the greater Saguaro scene back when he was killing it as an investigative journalist. Unfortunately, that lifestyle led Ben to snorting cocaine while alone, as a boost for a busy day or stressful event. Eventually, he was using it several times a day, every day; he became addicted and lost control. It was as a journalist conducting an award-winning investigation on how drugs were destroying society that Ben Morris came to be introduced to the term "Meth Mouth". It was ugly then, but even uglier now as Ben found himself with this wretched looking woman in a room that seemed like a 'Soviet era' confinement area awaiting your number to be called by the KGB.

Before Ben had a chance to sit down, Probation Officer Julio Chavez hollered out from the now open security door for Ben to come back to his office. That was bad enough, but when Ben heard Chavez's next words, his blood ran cold. "Ben Morris, I've been looking forward to chatting with you this morning, please come to my office!" said a crafty looking Julio Chavez, knowing he was scaring Ben Morris in such a way that only a professional tormentor could achieve. Ben Morris is now in Julio Chavez's lair.

"You know the drill Morris, piss test first," snarled Chavez. He continued, "Let's make it quick this time and don't even think about faking it with some holy man's piss because I'll be standing right behind you. Pull anything funny or even splash too much on the side of the toilet, you'll be cuffed up and headed back to county"

"I'm not going to try anything funny, I'm clean as a whistle and I've got good news Mr. Chavez", Ben enthusiastically says, hoping to set a positive tone.

"Save the bullshit for my office, I've got something to ask you, so hurry the fuck up!" An already irritated sounding Julio Chavez barked, intending to keep Morris off balance, which is clearly working as if he were able to read Ben's mind.

"Put the cup in the box and wash your fucking hands before touching anything. I'm a busy man and need to get on to more important things than crybaby criminals like you." Chavez delivers this last salvo while internally smiling at how well he's controlling case # PO1958.

Except for the inside of a county jail cell, there's no other place on earth that Ben Morris would rather not be than the office of Julio Chavez, Nazi Probation Officer extraordinaire. Just as Ben was about to blurt out his good news of a job and hopefully garner some approval, he's totally surprised when Chavez asks him; "So Morris, tell me what you think about that cop, murder or suicide, what is it?"

Completely caught off guard, Ben is baffled by the question and he doesn't know how to respond. Thinking this must be some sort of trick, he finally says; "Sir, I'm not sure I'm following you; I honestly don't know what it is you're asking me."

"Oh fuck, come on man, the biggest story around, even the national media is running with it' and you don't know what I'm talking about?" Chavez says, clearly of the belief Morris is playing coy, confirming in his mind that Morris knows something and doesn't want to share.

"Seriously sir, I don't have a TV or a radio. There's a crappy one in the lobby of the "Del Vista", but I don't linger there for many reasons. I can't afford a newspaper and only use free fliers for the want ads. I suppose I got used to not following the news when I was in the lock-up, I never thought about it before now. I really don't know much about any current news. Christ, America might be at war again and I wouldn't know. That's not cool." Ben Morris replied, now actually concerned (scared in fact) about how internally focused he had become since his world fell apart.

Now an equally baffled, but still wary and suspicious Julio Chavez says, quietly and sincerely, "You really don't know what I'm talking about do you?

Ben simply shakes his head no and doesn't say a word.

"Jesus Christ, here all this time I thought the 'big shot' journalist could give me an inside track on what is becoming the story of the fucking decade, about a cop no less, but you apparently have escaped into your own mind and are living in the Disney Land castle, just fucking perfect."

Chavez continued, now with his more familiar angry tone, "Look Morris, I don't like you or people like you. Life came way too easy for you and then you blew it. I admit it, I laughed and was happy to see it happen because life doesn't often play it fair when the shit comes falling down, but this time it found a deserving target.

"On the other hand, I actually did admire some of your work as a reporter, you uncovered some good shit. Your work a few years back on the Saguaro police scandal exposing officers working off-duty security jobs and then back-billing the city for overtime pay? That was an eye-opener for sure and no one likes a dirty cop, I know I don't."

Ben was astonished. Chavez had even more to say, "Morris, you know how to dig deep into shit, either that or you have great unnamed sources, maybe both, not sure. I figured on this one you'd have an angle that could solve this mind puzzler for me since the dead cop was one you named in your investigation for God's sake, Kevin Galway...and you're telling me you didn't know that?"

Ben was stunned at hearing that name. He suddenly found himself thinking once again like a fierce investigative reporter and journalist. His curiosity piqued, no longer the scared rabbit fearing to be gobbled up by the fierce wolf, he now focused on gathering information. His PO unwittingly provided a new source of hope for Ben, though neither of the men fully understood the implications yet.

"I need you to tell me everything you know about the case, but first I want to inform you that I have a job starting Saturday." Ben had purposely left out the details because for the first time since meeting PO Julio Chavez, he was in control.

"Oh? Hey, good work on finding a job dude, I'll get it documented. Now, let me tell you what I know about the case, it's a strange one…." Julio Chavez continued, never realizing he had forever lost his leverage over Ben Morris.

{ CHAPTER 6 }

Coffee, Cops and Questions

It was early morning and as cool as it's going to get for the day. It's also Saturday, which means no school and that Resource Police Officer Marcus Johnson could enjoy the next two days off. Most cops work a 4 day on, 3 day off, 10 hour shift, rotating schedule. School resource officer's maintain a more classic 8 hour day, 5 days a week schedule to match the normal hours of the school. For many cops, especially those that no longer want to face the hard dangers of the profession, especially on the mean streets where crime never seems to take a day off, this can be a near perfect assignment. For Marcus Johnson, it's more of a place to hide from his past days of wearing a badge, but it's not from fear of the streets. What Marcus Johnson is hiding from is something he can't fight or fix, unless he could find a handy time machine and go back in time, which is not likely to happen.

Up until just recently, his seeking out specific job assignments seemed to be the perfect way of keeping him where he needed to be, both physically and emotionally, but the news about his old colleague, squad mate and one time friend Kevin Galway has changed everything for Marcus. Bad feelings he once believed he could always suppress, combined now with new dark thoughts have taken over in a way that leaves him feeling out of control....probably the same way Galway felt. Having only slept off-and-on briefly over the last couple of nights, he could use some hot coffee and a scone or muffin; the stereo-type of a cop eating a doughnut is an image he can't deal with, because right now he hates even being a cop. It's cool outside, still in the low 90's, a walk down to the 'Hippie' fair at the park for some caffeine, hoping the shitheads are still asleep, this seems like a good plan. These are the thoughts of conflicted police officer Marcus Johnson who desperately seeks a place of peace wherever he can find it.

It's 7AM or 0700 by Marcus Johnson's way of thinking when he entered the green space known as the "Sandra-Rose Vance" Memorial Park, more commonly referred to simply as 'Vance Park'. It had been dedicated to a long passed mayor of Saguaro, Arizona, who was credited with having the vision of allowing industry and growth to 'transform' the city into a modern place of commerce and power. Critics will counter she allowed big money to ruin the city, paying her to look the other way while sky scrapers were erected with little to no thought as to the impact of things like traffic congestion, air pollution, water usage, city services, displacements of citizens, etc.; there is truth to both assessments. Unfortunately, on most days, the park generally caters to transients, drunks and crack/meth heads. On Saturday's though, especially early, the undesirables are driven out by the many marketers and businesses trying to make a buck with coffee, food, trinkets, music, tattoos, piercings, and 60's style fares like incense, shirts, hats, ribbons and bells.

Marcus remains focused on his top priority, finding some coffee and heads to the first trailer he sees, "Bathsheba's Rainbow Bistro", sounds as good as any. Looking around, he figures he'll need the caffeine jolt to push him through this crowd of clowns. With a deep sigh, he heads up to the shiny stainless counter of the trailer and orders a cup of high strength black coffee and an actually delicious looking muffin from a face he knows, because most good cops, even those that no longer want to be one, they don't forget faces. Well hello, 'fallen from grace' Ben Morris! This is not at all what Marcus expected this morning.

As the coffee and muffin are placed on the stainless steel counter, before asking how much he owed for his soon to be breakfast, Marcus Johnson delivers an unexpected question; "So, let me guess, the dark, ugly underbelly of the barista trade is finally going to be exposed?"

A clearly confused Ben Morris, finally responds with a question of his own; "What are you talking about?"

"Don't worry man, I'm not going to blow your cover or anything, these coffee shops with their fancy mobile trailers have always seemed shady to me, I just hope you can get to the bottom of it and make it out alive, there's some scary looking dudes wearing those aprons!", says Marcus Johnson, who is struggling to cover up a huge smile, something he hasn't even considered doing for the last few weeks.

At seeing Johnson's extremely poor 'poker face', Ben realized he was being played, this guy obviously recognized him from somewhere, most likely from his TV days based on the smartass question. "I get it now, you recognize me, but should I know you, or better yet, how exactly do you know me?" a cautious Ben asks.

"Well, besides the fact I'm the only black man in this park, at least for now, but very likely the only one you'll have as a customer, I'm also a cop and I'm good with faces." Marcus admits and then continues, "When you were on channel 14, you did a number on some of my colleagues over some overtime pay issues, I'm guessing every cop in the county, maybe even the state knows your face and name Mr. Morris."

"Don't worry though, I'm not out for vengeance, several of those guys were dirty, but unfortunately some weren't, yet in the end they were all lumped together. Did you know that none of them were ever fired? One left by way of retirement, but all your hard charging investigative report did was result in a couple of internal suspensions, some loss of pay and the general public coming away thinking cops are criminals wearing a uniform with a badge."

"That was never my intention, Officer...?" responded a now piqued Ben Morris.

Surprising even himself, Marcus says, "My name is Marcus Johnson and I'm not pulling your leg about being a cop, but I don't know how long that's going to be the case. My being a cop I mean."

The now curious Ben Morris asks, “Officer Johnson, would you be willing to meet later after I’m finished here? I need answers to some questions and I have the strange feeling you do too.”

“What time do you get off work?” Johnson asks, not exactly sure what he might be getting himself into, but he does have questions about many things right now and zero answers.

{ CHAPTER 7 }

Saguaro PD Crime Lab, Main Police Headquarters

Whoosh! The sound made when anyone crosses in or out of the environmentally controlled spaces of the Saguaro PD crime lab. Entering the space at the moment is the Supervising Crime Lab Technician, Bill Winters. He's been summoned by one of the younger crime lab techs, an extremely competent, but equally nerdy individual who says he has news about a cache of weapons that had been found by a young home owner attempting to plant a tree several months ago during the Spring. As with most large city police departments, crime labs are staffed with civilian employees, technicians and scientists who conduct the clinical and forensic examinations and testing of evidence found at a crime scene, including objects and weapons of all sorts.

Because the science has become so advanced, the technicians have the ability to confirm if a gun has been fired, can match the gun to spent casings, complete bullets and even in some cases, partial fragments. Fingerprinting, blood-typing, DNA recovery, ballistic testing, are how court cases are won, how criminals are put away and how justice is properly served. Well, that's what the lab techs always say, out of earshot of any sworn peace officer of course, because most cops would likely have a very different opinion on the subject. In fact, some of the cops they interact with, the ones who actually deal face-to-face with the gun toting, knife wielding criminals, they can be a bit scary at times, no need to start a feud. Lab techs are quick to mention though that on TV, forensic crime shows often get better ratings over reality shows filming actual police calls. In their minds, this confirmed that science was the true foundation of effective law enforcement.

"Okay Jenkins, I got your text, were you able to recover a serial number off one of those rusty guns?" A very busy Bill Winters asks.

"Please Bill, you know my name is Randall, we're not in the Army and calling out my last name will draw half of Nebraska if you aren't careful....but no, I didn't find any serial numbers. They were all ground off as expected." A perturbed Randall Jenkins states and then continues on excitedly, "However, I did recover a partial smudged palm print, unusable, but also one distinctly clear thumb print!"

A disbelieving Bill Winters simply says, "How? Those guns were in the ground a long time, damp and rusty, there's no way prints could've survived on them!"

"Correct Bill, as always!" a smiling Randall Jenkins answered, before quickly continuing, "The guns didn't have any prints *on* them, but inside them! One had a still greased ammo magazine that was inserted in an AK-47!"

A silent Bill Winters pulls up a rolling chair and sits down, thinking this could be a major break. "Cut to the chase Jenk, er, Randall, were you able to match the print?"

"YES!" Randall responds loudly.

"So, you made a match through AFIS?" AFIS being a national data base of all criminals with fingerprint records, managed by the Department of Justice, allowing access to all law enforcement agencies. AFIS in fact enjoys reciprocated shared access between INTERPOL and other allied international agencies.

Randall responded back with a surprise answer, "No Bill, not exactly. I found the match right here in the Saguaro City data bank, the thumb print is from one of ours."

Immediately frustrated Bill Winters blurts out, "Oh Jesus, please don't tell me one of those rookie cops on the recovery scene handled the weapon without gloves. I'm hearing from everyone lately that the most recent crop of recruits coming out of the academy, they just aren't cutting it. Damn it to hell!"

"No, wait Bill, when I said not exactly, I meant that the print is in fact from a Saguaro police officer, but he's been dead for nearly 20 years." Randall fell silent after delivering his news.

Bill Winters stands up and says, "Bring your information, we need to go talk to the Sergeant, this doesn't seem right and I'm not sure I want to write it into a report just yet."

* * *

Sergeant Vernon (Vern) Kerley tells both Bill Winters and Randall Jenkins to sit across from him at his desk. Young Jenkins was clearly in awe of the situation. Vern Kerley was a rarity in the Saguaro PD because he actually has a walled office, not a cubicle like most PD sergeants. The operation he oversaw dealt with critical data and information that if leaked, could damage cases being tried by the County Attorney's office, and potentially violate every privacy law imaginable. Hence the need for a secure enclosed space.

There was a time when Vern, as a street cop sneered at anyone working a desk, like he's been doing for some time now. When he was younger, the job seemed binary; good guys versus bad guys. After 28 years, moving from the street to the detective corps and eventually into the crime lab, Vern has seen enough to blur that binary vision. Sometimes cops get it wrong, but data and science, when properly applied, it doesn't lie.

Vern knows Bill Winters to be a competent square shooter, someone he depends on more than he wants to openly admit. Cops rarely, if ever, fully trust an unsworn co-worker, but Vern long ago made an exception for Bill.

On the other hand, the millennial puke Randall Jenkins reminds Vern of his oldest sister's son, another worthless, millennial with a 'man bun', constantly talking about the oppression of Blacks, Hispanics, Native Americans and other peoples of color, a terrible state of affairs, which oddly enough, he does not extend to Asians, go figure.

Unlike Randall Jenkins, his nephew has never had a job. After achieving not one, but two degrees, from an expensive out-of-state university, he has since lived at home with his recently widowed mother. Secretly, Vernon would dearly love to grab his nephew by his 'man bun', sling him from the mandatory "Thanksgiving table", slamming him into a wall and telling him, 'up close and personal', that because of him, his dad died out of disappointment and debt. As pleasant as that thought might be, spilling gravy on his sister's table cloth would not be a good thing.

"What do you boys have for me?" Vern asked, hoping it was a breakthrough on an ugly, unsolved serial rape situation in north Saguaro, which was currently being covered by all local media sources, but could break nationally unless it was quickly resolved.

Bill Winters piped up quickly, not giving the excited Randall Jenkins a chance to speak, "We got a print and a match from that load of buried guns from a few months back."

A skeptical Sergeant Kerley countered with a question, "How is that possible Bill, those guns were rusted and buried for years? You can't get prints off rusted guns, you know that. What are you trying to sell here?"

"No sir, it wasn't *on* one of the guns, it was from an ammo magazine in one of the AK-47 rifles that preserved a print because of the packing grease!" This was the overly excited Lab Tech Jenkins, loudly blurting out the news, all while being deftly restrained by a hand from Bill Winters, which kept him from jumping up from his chair.

Bill verbally takes control and says, "Well Sergeant, it's not from a criminal, it's actually a confirmed print from a Saguaro PD officer."

"So, it's scene contamination then?" The obvious answer Vernon expected to sadly hear.

Again, Randall excitedly prattled, "No sir, the print matches clearly to officer David Chiang, but our records indicate he's been dead nearly 20 years, but it's a definitive match, verified by multiple methods."

This isn't news Vernon was expecting at all, so unexpected in fact, it caused him to let down his guard. Before he realized it, he quietly, but clearly said; "The Four Horsemen".

"Four Horsemen, isn't that from the bible or something? No wait, I remember my grandfather saying his dad talked about 'Four Horsemen' on a football team....was that the Raiders maybe, I don't follow sports?" Randall Jenkins asks.

Vern, realizing his mistake recovered quickly, enthusiastically congratulating Jenkins on his find, assuring him the thumb print was likely from a gun that the late Officer David Chiang must have touched during a previous confiscation from criminals at some time in the past. Then Vern shared info with both Jenkins and Bill Winters, the details of an ugly city incident.

Many years back, in the south precinct, a police vehicle full of confiscated weapons had been staged, awaiting transport to the old downtown arsenal for further forensic examination. The guns that were not to be used as evidence or returned to their rightful owners, they would eventually be auctioned off, as was policy in those days.

Then the worst possible scenario came about; the police transport vehicle and the weapons were stolen from the precinct parking yard. This was all true, but Sgt. Vern Kerley did not share that this event had gone much further than embarrassment, as careers had been affected. Many higher- ranking officers had suddenly taken retirement. Suspensions and loss of pay penalties were extended to many throughout the ranks, whether they had direct responsibility or not, yet no one had actually been fired.

This was a highly guarded secret within the Saguaro police department; the press would have destroyed them were it to leak out. Vern Kerley was not about to start now, especially after what that asshole from Channel 14 did a couple of years ago over some overtime bullshit. Vern instructed both Randall Jenkins and Bill Winters to keep this old information strictly confidential, like most everything else that happened within the crime lab. Both men nodded, indicating their understanding of the instruction.

"Mr. Jenkins, this is some very good work, thank you! I'll do some follow-up, but what I really need you to do now is review the evidence the officers and detectives have brought in on that north-side rapist case, we have to bring this to a rapid close." Vern knew how to hit the right buttons quite easily. He had become more of a politician than a cop now, something that bothered him deeply.

"Yes sir, Sergeant Kerley! We were recently sent in a knife for testing, I'll get right on it!" Randall Jenkins said, beaming with pride.

"Again, thanks for the good work. Bill, I need you to hang back a bit, I want to discuss another case" Vern said, clearly indicating that Randall Jenkins was now dismissed.

Once Jenkins shut the door behind him, Vern said, "Bill, I need you to do a couple of things. Have your boys fire that AK-47, the one the print was found in, and run ballistics on the recovered round." Then, clearing his throat, continued, "Along with that, I also need you to dig into some old records about a shooting where a cop died. The name of the cop is Frank Garcia, he was one of ours. Find the ballistics report of the bullet recovered from his body. Compare it to the test fire you conduct. But Bill, I need to make this perfectly clear, whatever results you conclude, you provide them to me only, no one else, especially not that punk Jenkins, you understand me?" "Loud and clear sergeant, loud and clear"

{ CHAPTER 8 }

Vance Park Saguaro, Arizona, late at night

"I apologize for the location, I suppose this time of night, a bar would have been more appropriate. I'm not allowed to drink and frankly, I don't have enough money to pay for two cheap draft beers." Ben Morris embarrassingly admitted to Marcus Johnson, who was sitting across from him at a concrete park table with matching concrete bench seats.

Marcus responded by saying, "No worries, I don't trust myself in a bar or around a bottle right now…I start drinking and I might not stop. No this place is just fine." He continued, "So how are we going to do this? In fact, WHY are we doing this?" Pushing further, "As a cop, I'm used to being the one that asks the questions, but if I'm not mistaken, you're an investigative reporter, or at least used to be, shouldn't you be asking the questions?"

"Ha, that's a good observation Officer Johnson! In a sane world, you'd be right, but there's not been any sanity in my world for more than a year now. Frankly, I don't know exactly what I am now other than a part time flunky in a coffee shop owned by a scary looking lesbian." Ben says, smiling outwardly, but there is nothing funny inside him right now.

"Okay, fair enough" said Officer Johnson, "But call me Marcus, not officer Johnson, that's what the kids call me at school and these days I don't think I deserve the title." Then Marcus says, "Why are we here Mr. Morris?"

"First, make that Ben, Mr. Morris was my dad. You're right though about the question-asking protocol, but since your comments this morning and just now, I'm not sure you even consider yourself to be a cop, for some reason, and I don't know that I can say I'm an investigative reporter now, but it's what we've been accustomed to."

Ben continued after a pause, "The reason I initially wanted to talk to you is you told me you were a cop, I'm looking for some information that only a cop might be able to provide. Then, that old reporter 'breaking story' meter in my head went off when you let it slip you didn't know if you were going to be a cop for long."

"Marcus, why don't you think you'll be a cop for long, are you planning to quit?"

Marcus didn't answer, but asked a question instead, "What particular information are you looking for that I might have?"

Not hesitating, Ben asked, "Did Sergeant Kevin Galway kill himself?" Marcus simply sat without moving or speaking for several minutes as tears flowed down his face. Ben too sat in silence and nothing was said by either man.

After a very, long and uncomfortable period of time, the silence deafening, Marcus asks Ben, "Did you know Kevin and I were once good friends?"

"No, I didn't." Ben quietly said. "Did you have a falling out or something?"

Half snorting, smiling while wiping at his eyes, Marcus Johnson responded, "Or something… yeah, in fact, that's pretty accurate. We never officially declared to each other that we were no longer friends or anything formal, that never happened. Good friends though, they call each other, they talk, they meet up for a beer and visit on holidays, they go to ball games, I mean, don't they Ben, in your world?"

Ben did not answer.

"Kevin and I didn't do that, at least not for nearly the last 20 years. There was a time we were like brothers. I know cops say that all the time, but few truly believe it. In this case it was true, and it wasn't just me and Kevin, there were two others, four of us, a true 'band of brothers'."

Ben said nothing, waiting for Marcus to speak again, which he did.

"Ben, why are you asking about Kevin? Please tell me you're not wanting to drag his name into the dirt, because if that's what you intend to do, I won't ever help you. In fact I will hurt you more than you can ever imagine."

A contrite Ben answered, "No Marcus, that's not my intention at all. He was one of the cops in my story related to the overtime scam. I want to know if that might have led him to commit suicide. Or was he killed by someone? I feel an obligation to him and his family if he has one."

Ben continued, "I didn't even know about his death until my dick of a probation officer grilled me about it. He thought because of my journalistic past, I'd have some answers to the mystery. Marcus, I can't even get a job in any TV, radio or newspaper business cleaning toilets for God's sakes. I've been completely blacklisted. This is personal. I don't want a man's death on my conscience. I don't know if I can live with that possibility."

After a moment of silence, Marcus finally speaks, "I don't really know if Kevin killed himself or not, I wasn't there. What I do know is that having the death of someone weighing on your heart is crazy hard…if that's your reason, I'll help you, but it's complicated."

"Complicated, how?" Ben asked.

"It's a very long story. The only way you'll understand is if I take you back to the beginning. I've relived it a million times in my mind and it still doesn't make sense to me, but maybe it will for you if I tell it. You want to hear the story Ben? Do you think it will help clear your conscience? I hope it does, I really do, but don't get your hopes up."

Ben is now deep inside himself in a way he had not been since languishing in jail, after weeks of shedding the enslaving yoke of cocaine and alcohol when he could finally think clearly again.

"Marcus, I want to hear the story, all of it, but tell me straight, why are you willing to do this? It isn't just about helping me clear my conscience. There has to be more to it. So why Marcus, really…why?

While eye-locked with Ben, Marcus truthfully declares, "If I don't tell someone, I'll be as dead as Kevin Galway, except there'll be no mystery about it; my issued sidearm will still be in my hand and the top of my head plastered on the ceiling of my condo."

{ CHAPTER 9 }

Meet the Four Horsemen

It was early June of 1999 in Saguaro, Arizona, just as the temperatures rocket to something commonly found on the surface of the sun. Sane people seek air conditioning and shade during such times, but for roughly 50 individuals, that's not part of the plan. These people have as their goal in life, to wear a uniform, carry a badge and enforce the law. Their dreams were easier to achieve in slumber than in reality because sitting before them now is the entry point to the Arizona Combined Law Enforcement Academy, more commonly known by the acronym, "ACLEA".

This very serious institution sat atop the foothills located adjacent to the southern mountain barrier that defined the city of Saguaro Arizona. It's a difficult academy to pass, but especially during the summer months. The heat alone, much less the stress of the acumen will cause a good number to drop out during the first few days, while still others will quit throughout the long process. Fashioned much like the military basic training process, the academy takes those similar elements of testing and qualification, all while melding law enforcement focus into the process. Upon successful completion of the academy, graduates should be able to shoot proficiently, run, fight, drive fast with deft effectiveness, but also be armed with a deep understanding of the law and how it pertains to properly enforce those laws. At least that's the goal of the academy administrators and trainers.

In 1999, there were only a handful of female candidates. For the ones that didn't quit after two days, the remaining women recruits, although expected to meet the same physical standards as their male counterparts, the trainers often looked the other way and graded with a much more forgiving hand, which didn't go unnoticed. The male recruits would grumble about it amongst themselves in the shower and locker rooms, but they reluctantly accepted the double standard. Being a 'combined academy' for the state, there were recruits from multiple agencies, from the biggest cities like Saguaro, to some very small towns and the disparity was hard to ignore. Saguaro originally had more than a dozen recruits enter the academy, but when all was said and done, only 8 remained standing on graduation day. Some small towns funded only one entrant.

To the credit of the small agency entrants, they passed all challenges from the beginning to the end and generally were embraced by their class. Unfortunately, the 'scuttlebutt' amongst the recruits, was that 'front money' ensured the small town 'heroes' would make it, no matter what. Hearing those rumors and observing the lax 'unofficial' grading standards for females, certain male recruits, who were quickly immersing themselves into the 'cop' way of thinking, this flew into the face of what honest law enforcement was supposed to be. It was during this time that four recruits forged a bond that would continue past the academy.

The next stop after graduation was Field Training, referred to generally as "FTO" training. FTO is an introduction to what most sane people would consider a nightmare, but to academy graduates, now with a badge, this was a dream come true.

Of the 8 Saguaro AZ recruits that had passed the academy, they are dispersed to precincts across the city that most needed officers. It just so happened, that the actual physical acreage that ACLEA was built upon was in one of the worst crime ridden areas of Saguaro. Four new officers will do their Field Training in the "Southern Vista" police precinct. David Chiang, Marcus Johnson, Frank Garcia and Kevin Galway all found themselves happily assigned to the same precinct, especially to be in the 'hottest' crime area of the city. These four men had bonded during the grueling training elements of ACLEA. In their minds, this wasn't the result of a random selection process. Each of them firmly believed they were brought together to serve as a team by an unknown force. If fate had bonded them during the academy and had now brought them together again in FTO, they felt an obligation to do their best to pass this next test. Only then can they get out on the street to deliver justice as they feel is their destiny to fulfill. Nearly 2 months later, all four officers are successful in passing Field Training and initially three of them are assigned to the same squad; Chiang, Johnson and Galway. Six months later, when the first opportunity to transfer (the police term being 'drop paper'), Officer Frank Garcia joined his brothers in blue. The team was back together again.

Not just together, but making good impressions with their work ethic, motivation and willingness to 'get into shit' as cops call it; meaning they proactively dig into criminal activity and never hold back from addressing dangerous situations. When their aggressive tactics begin to provide Homicide, Robbery, Narcotics and Gang detectives with persons of interest, along with evidence and crucial information, it doesn't go unnoticed. Some older cops begin to refer to the rookie attention grabbers as "The Four Horsemen" and it sticks. Intended as a disparaging slight, it soon grows amongst the department and with the criminal element as well because the "Horsemen" were making so many arrests and solving cases, they were hard to ignore.

As for the four officers in question, they clearly enjoyed the notoriety. Their individual egos would soar when interrogating a suspect and if the name "Four Horseman" was invoked, the scared facial expressions, followed by immediate cooperation, it was intoxicating to the young cops. Even observing threatening "Horsemen" graffiti show up on buildings and fences had been a quiet source of pride for the young cops, not realizing that it was at the same time a source of professional envy and disdain by many older cops. Vanity aside, there had been little question as to the quality and quantity of work being produced by this young group of officers. Their arrest statistics alone told the story and command staff took full advantage of it. Through these times, the young 'band of brothers' stuck together tightly.

The ultimate indication of their strong bond with each other came when Garcia designed a drawing based on a biblical version of 'The Four Horsemen of the Apocalypse'. Each officer had it tattooed on their chest. Soon, the operational environment changed drastically as drug Cartels from Mexico began operating and nothing would ever be the same.

* * *

Back in the present, hidden in a darkened area of Vance Park, the fair over, it was now early Sunday morning and the park was reverting back to what it normally is; a dangerous place to be, especially during such early hours.

Marcus Johnson asked the lone audience member, Ben Morris, an odd question under the circumstances. "Ben, are you a religious man or have you at least read the bible? "

As if a spell has been suddenly broken, Ben says, "No, on both counts actually. I come from a family of non-practicing Jews." "Although in college I did have to take a mandatory religious studies class as part of my journalism curriculum," he added, hoping it was a helpful response.

"In that class, did you hear the reference, 'Four Horsemen of the Apocalypse' from the New Testament as described in the book of Revelations?" Marcus asks.

Ben shook his head yes and said, "Yeah, something about the bringing of plagues and bad stuff during the end times or something to that effect I think, but I don't really know for sure."

"Yeah, that's close enough. In the bible they were actually talked about in both the Old and New Testament, but in any case they represented bad shit happening, usually resulting in death. Each Horseman Ben, they brought it in different ways."

Marcus continued on while chuckling, "When my granny was alive back in Georgia, she'd scare us kids by saying those 'White Horsemans', they gonna come down and getchu if you disbehave! We'd work hard not to laugh about her pronunciation of words because if she saw us snickering, she'd likely take a switch to our hides, but that's only if she could ever catch one of us....! "

No longer chuckling or smiling, Marcus, suddenly declared, "It's dangerous here. We need to go and when we do, stay by me, I'm armed."

"If you want to hear the rest of the story, we'll need to meet again so I'm going to give you my phone number on a card, you call me. This gives you and me both some time to decide if what we're doing really has a purpose, because right now, dredging all this up isn't giving me the relief I was hoping for, but....well, there's a lot more to be said."

Ben turns to Marcus and puts out a hand suddenly stopping him, "NO! I mean, yeah we clearly need to leave this place. I feel eyes on my back. I mean no, don't stop telling me the story. I'll figure out a place where we can talk, I want to hear the rest, can we do that?"

Marcus simply nods in the affirmative. As they approach a park light, he pulls out a blank index card, commonly carried by cops to document case notes. In this particular case, it's for the number of Marcus's cell phone, which he writes down and hands to Ben.

"Thank you Marcus, I'll call soon, believe me I will, but I have one question I need an answer to right now; how many of the Four Horsemen remain?"

Marcus stared hard at Ben before finally answering. "Only one left Ben. It's me. Horsemen bring death and I'll need to turn in my saddle soon."

{ CHAPTER 10 }

Bistro business

On Monday morning, in Saguaro, Ben Morris walked to "Bathsheba's Rainbow Bistro" for two reasons; he needed his fifty dollars from Saturday's work at Vance Park, and he needs a favor. He hopes Shelley Conner will provide both. As he entered the place, which was actually much larger inside than from what it looked from the sidewalk, Ben immediately saw the owner, Shelley Conner. Shelley, upon seeing Ben, loudly said in front of several customers, grabbing their attention, "I figured you'd show up soon enough. Jesus said you did a good job, but I didn't get a single phone call from any sweet-ass girls, not a one, so maybe I should dock your pay?"

Worried, Ben quietly replied, while walking directly toward her, uncomfortably avoiding the stares of the customers, "No, please Shelley, there weren't any opportunities. Really, I would have had them call you if there were."

"Come on pretty boy, I'm just busting your balls a bit, ease up, I have your $50 right here and want you back next Saturday at the park. In fact, based on the glowing performance report I got, I'm thinking maybe we can find some things for you to do here in the store 2 or 3 days a week."

"Oh. Well, yeah, that's great. Um, thank you." Ben said, so focused on his real issue now: a place to finish his talk with Marcus Johnson in private. The idea of employment has surprisingly taken a lower priority.

"Well don't knock yourself out with appreciation asshole, I just offered you a job, something I thought you wanted and needed. Maybe you really don't." Shelley snarled while closing the distance between her and Ben.

A now fully attentive Ben Morris quickly replied, "NO, NO, NO, Shelley, thank you so much, and YES, I'll start anywhere, anytime, please, I'm so sorry!" Any employment you can provide me is a blessing and I promise I'll do my best!"

Skeptically Shelley asked, "What's your issue then, you look like the IRS is on your ass, but you don't have any money, so what is it kid?"

Ben responded, "I need a place to talk privately with a man I met and I'm asking if I can do it here, will you let me?"

Shelley, wide-eyed, said, "Good Christ Morris, I was only joking when I suggested the 'boys in the county jail' turned you, but apparently it wasn't a joke. Sure, you bring your boyfriend and 'chat' all you need to, just don't chat so much Jesus has to mop up anything from your 'conversation'."

"Shelley, first thank you for the employment opportunity, I need it, badly and also for allowing me a place to talk, it's important, I appreciate it more than you know. Second, the man I need to talk to, it's not what you think, I'm not into men and I'm not being judgmental, it's just not my thing, this is about something different."

Eying him closely, Shelley questioned "What are you up to kid, are you in trouble with the law? I can't be bringing that kind of shit down on me, not now after finally getting this place operating in the black."

Ben shook his head no, saying, "No, not in trouble with the law, but it does have something to do with the law in a roundabout way, nothing that will bring you any grief whatsoever. Shelley, I'm not sure exactly what it is I'm dealing with, at least not yet, but my instincts tell me that if I don't get involved, someone might die and I can't let that happen. I'm scared I might have already been responsible for one death and never even realized it. I need to find out for sure and do what I can to make it right."

Arms folded across her ample chest, Shelley Conner said, with stern sarcasm, "I remember now why I prefer the company of girls and swore off pretty boys like you 30 plus years ago…yet people still think women are the drama queens of the world, Geezus Pleezus!

"Okay Superhero, meet and talk with your friend, but I need you here at 7AM on Wednesday, Thursday and Friday, then at the park on Saturday by 5AM. Will that fit your busy life-saving schedule?"

Smiling with sincerity, Ben simply replied, "Thank you."

"Be careful Ben, whatever it is you're doing." It's the first time she had ever called Ben Morris by his first name. Shelley is worried and it bothers her. She had somehow let another 'pretty boy' interrupt her life, something she swore would never be allowed to happen again.

{ Chapter 11 }

Phones, fame and shame

Ben Morris was happy, but he realized he faced a technical problem, he doesn't own a cell phone. He had one before he entered the Hohokam County jail system. Unfortunately, his state of mind facing incarceration, along with being drug-addled, it had left him clueless as to what happened to his phone and where it might be now. He's not sure if he was actually carrying it when taken into custody in the court room or if he had given it to someone, maybe his lawyer? That's not an inquiry he wants to make. Ben's attorney, although initially hired, ended up being declared a public defender, an unusual situation.

Ann Warnyk came recommended as a defense attorney who was known to take on cases at reasonable rates. Ben had thought a defense attorney to be an affordable upgrade over a public defender. Early after his arrest, he initially treated it as some sort of joke, but after meeting with his lawyer, she had informed him it was very serious, he might be sent to prison. Shortly after the meeting, the television station he been reporting for released a public statement announcing his firing, making it clear that 'Ben Morris's actions do not comport with or are in any way considered to be acceptable'. Almost immediately, his once vibrant social circle had abandoned him. That was when Ben actually realized he was in serious trouble, with little money and no one he could ask to borrow from. He had then proceeded to use his remaining funds to score cocaine, pushing through the new stage of life in a perpetual blur.

The collapse of Ben Morris, investigative reporter, had morphed into a complete free fall. He informed his attorney of his financial reality, expecting her to drop him and cut ties like everyone else. To his complete surprise, she had informed him she would stay on 'pro bono', but would have to declare this financial arrangement to the court. This had been an odd and not often used legal technicality, through which Ann Warnyk would be listed as the public defender representing Ben. When he asked why she had done this, she responded that she had admired his work. Ben had smugly thought her to be just another one of his many groupies, so he had not questioned it. After a couple of months in the county jail, sobered from going 'cold turkey' from cocaine and alcohol, Ben had been ashamed to think of his incarceration and how he had dismissed her true kindness, believing he had been doing her a favor. As such, he had never requested any client-attorney phone calls that had been allowed him under the law. He also refused the many calls Amy had made to the jail, wanting to speak to him. Ben's shame was just too great.

Even after serving six months of a 1-year sentence, due to good behavior and successful completion of a drug rehab program, he still can't face her. Without a cell phone, his only options were pay phones, if he was lucky enough to find one these days or the desk phone at the Del Vista building where he was living, but the pleading and bribing necessary wasn't worth the effort. Ben did consider one other outside option; to borrow a cell phone.

A surprising number of the occupants in his building, some that looked like they'd be better suited living out of a shopping cart, they actually had cell phones. When asked how they got them, most didn't seem to know or refused to answer. A couple did mumble that the 'welfare people' gave it to them. Later today he would need a phone to call Marcus Johnson, hoping he will be willing to meet at Bathsheba's to continue their conversation. Marcus told him he worked as a school resource officer, so he wouldn't attempt a call during the day. He wouldn't be able to leave a message because he had no return number to call. He decided he would wait until 6PM. If Johnson was out, he would try again at 7PM. He knew of a pay phone in the lobby of a nearby hotel that didn't have security guards and stayed open until midnight, that's where he would try.

* * *

At 6PM, Ben called the number on the card he got from Marcus. To his surprise and relief Johnson answered after 2 simulated rings.

"Yeah", was all that Johnson said.

"Marcus, this is Ben Morris, we talked on Saturday night, you recall giving me your number?"

"Yeah, I remember", Marcus responded, but offered nothing else.

Ben quickly followed, "You said you had more to tell me about things that seemed to be important to you and they might be for me as well, are you still willing to meet so we can talk?"

After a long silence, Marcus said, "I did a lot of thinking since we met and told myself you'd never call, which was probably for the best. But, if you did call, I'd meet and talk. So where and when? It can't be on Thursday, I have a funeral to attend, a cop funeral."

Ben realized two things: the funeral must be for Kevin Galway and he had forgotten to tell Shelley Conner that he had to meet with his probation officer on Thursday. DAMN IT!

Now flustered, Ben responded by saying, "How about now, say 7PM at Bathsheba's Bistro, I sort of work there, but we'd just be regular customers."

"Congratulations, I'm sure the benefits package is awesome. I'll be there, no secret handshakes or anything like that. Do they have food, something besides muffins? I haven't had anything to eat all day, I need more than coffee." Marcus asked.

"Well, I think they make sandwiches, but I'm not sure. I guess I better find out now that I work there." Ben admitted.

Ben had his meeting locked in, but was unsure what he would hear and why he was willing to hear it. He wanted to put his shame to rest and regain his dignity. If it did turn out that a cop killed himself because of Ben's reporting, he wasn't sure he could live with the truth.

{ CHAPTER 12 }

Cops, coffee and confessions

"Morris, what the hell are Rainbow Snaps?" asked Marcus Johnson as he eyed the ordering board high on a wall behind the counter at "Bathsheba's Rainbow Bistro". "If they're anything similar to a bag of chips, I'd buy some to go with my sandwich...you work here, what are they?"Ben Morris meekly responded, "I'm not sure exactly, I've never actually worked in the store yet and they weren't on the menu last Saturday at the park. That was all coffee and breakfast stuff. I can ask."

A young, heavily pierced, and tattooed buxom girl with green hair working the counter was busy stacking cups and checking on the brewing pots.

"Uh, miss, I was wondering, um, the Rainbow Snaps, are they like a potato chip sort of thing that would go good with a sandwich?" Ben asked, uncomfortably, unsure why it is he felt like an orphaned boy at a social event. He had used to dine in the most expensive places the city had to offer, ordering and tipping like a Mafia Don. "Yeah, pretty much. They don't come in plastic bags like you get at a store. We fry them here fresh to order in the kitchen. You want to order some?" The surprisingly friendly sounding girl asked.

Before Ben could respond, Marcus authoritatively said, "Actually we'll have two orders and two Turkey Club sandwiches to go with it. To drink, I want to try the 'Iced Bathsheba Bomber', same for you Ben? I'm paying."

Stunned, Ben simply mutters, "Uh, yeah. That sounds really good, thanks."

The girl wrote down the order and before she turns, Marcus added, "This here is Ben Morris, he's famous and he works here too, but you probably haven't met him yet because he's working undercover, so please don't let that out, otherwise his case is over."

The girl, eyes and mouth wide open said, "That is so fucking cool, just like that undercover boss show on TV!" Before Ben could respond, she followed up with, "Everyone knows me as 'Tats'; that came from 'Tats has Tits', but they shortened it. I won't say anything to anyone, Oh God, this is so AWESOME! I can't wait to tell Jesus and Shelley!" A jubilant 'Tats' said as she ran to the back.

Snickering, Marcus, remarked, "Well so much for keeping it on the down-low!"

Sitting at a booth toward the back of the bistro, Ben said, "I don't understand you Marcus. One minute you come off as being so deep into a dark place you might not come back, then with the flick of a switch, you turn into the class clown, suddenly making jokes and fun, what gives?

Shaking his head in the affirmative, Marcus responded, "That's fair. That's actually a good observation in fact, like a good cop or investigative reporter would make. In my business, criminals often wear a mask to hide who they are, a disguise. Humor can be a very effective mask to disguise who you are; it's a good way to hide."

"So, is that what you're doing Marcus, hiding?" Ben asked.

"I suppose I am, but I'm not sure how much longer my mask is going to hold up." Marcus said without a hint of humor in his voice or expression.

"What exactly is it you're hiding from?" A deeply curious Ben asked.

"For starters, shame, guilt, deceit...I could add more to the list, but I'll stop there."Then Marcus continued, "I'm guessing I'm not the only person to have hid from the same things, in fact I'm sure of it. Have you ever known anyone like that Ben?"

Feeling as if he'd just been stung, Ben simply replied, "Yes, I have. What's the next step then?"

"I'm going to tell you a story and I want to do it now, tonight. I want it behind me. I can eat and talk at the same time and I'm assuming you can eat and listen at the same time, right?" Marcus received a nod from Ben and he waded right into it. Ben was going to learn things he never imagined about Marcus Johnson, which will give him reason to reconsider his thoughts about the death of Kevin Galway.

{ Chapter 13 }

The plan of all plans

By early 2001, in the Southern Vista Precinct, crime had been on the rise despite the best efforts of The Four Horsemen and other motivated officers. There had been a change; the drug busts were no longer relegated to personal use issues, but had grown to encompass distribution and transportation of marijuana, cocaine, heroin and methamphetamine. Another aspect had been the additional element of human smuggling. Large numbers of illegal aliens from south of the US border had increasingly been confined in houses throughout the city, until forced north and east throughout the country. Before that, illegal aliens weren't uncommon, but they had not previously been indentured as mules by the cartels. The Border Patrol actually monitored the radio channels of Saguaro PD for reports of persons of interest that were suspected to be in the country illegally. The Border Patrol would respond to assess the situation, taking custody of those who couldn't produce documentation confirming legal immigration status, unless a violent crime had been committed. In those cases, the police would take priority related to the crime, and legal status would be a secondary matter. Within a few short years, due to political pressures, the cooperation between local, state, and federal agencies regarding immigration law would be forced to end.

This increasingly volatile criminal activity had been solely attributed to Mexican Drug Cartels. They hadn't feared their own government because of the tremendous amounts of money to be made. Cartels had also been warring against each other for control of territories that offered entry into the US. Due to its proximity and desolation, the desert border of southern Arizona had been a prime target. Their brutal methods had quickly spread north into the US to protect the cargo they were trafficking. Anyone getting in their way could only expect the worst. This new brand of criminal was heavily armed; semi-auto and full auto rifles were their trademark, a big step up from the typical street gang weapons that cops had been used to encountering. It hadn't taken long for the police to realize the game had changed. One of the 'Four Horsemen' would find out the hard way.

Patrol Officer David Chiang had spotted a sedan with heavily tinted windows leaving an apartment complex known for heavy drug use. It had also been known as an ambush zone because it had only one driveway in and out of the semi-circle-shaped two-story complex. Officers would not drive into the center of the complex except, in large numbers with multiple vehicles, in order to provide cover. Shockingly, fire department and EMS units would only enter the complex if and when multiple police units were available as escorts, even if the call for medical service did not involve criminal activity. Considering the track record of the property, any vehicle entering or exiting had been suspected of being involved with a crime, especially at 11PM. Chiang had pulled behind the vehicle that had exited the complex. It hadn't been speeding or evading, but had an expired registration tag on the license plate, enough Probable Cause or "PC" as the cops call it, to make a legal stop.

Chiang had turned on the flashing red and blue lights, indicating for the driver to stop the vehicle, which it had done. Officer Chiang himself had come to a stop, taking the time to radio in his location, reason for the stop and then began entering in the license plate number on his mobile terminal. He did not ask for backup because he knows it wouldn't be necessary. Because of the location of his traffic stop, he was confident that other squad members would already be in route. All of them are familiar with the area and automatically provide assistance whether needed or not. Chiang confirmed the vehicle had not been stolen and radioed back to dispatch that he was going to talk to the driver.

Before he had even finished his radio transmission, the rear passenger door flew open and a male subject jumped out, firing a rifle at Chiang through his patrol vehicle's windshield. Chiang then immediately opened his door, crouched down and behind the engine compartment, using it as a shield. Another vicious volley of rifle rounds struck the police vehicle, before suddenly coming to a stop. Believing he had a chance to engage with his sidearm, still in a squatted position, Chiang carefully peered around the front of the squad car and saw the shooter with rifle in hand, not shooting, but trying to do something with the receiver of the rifle. Chiang believed the shooter was reloading, so he moved from his cover and fired several rounds, aiming at the shooter's center of mass. As the gunman fell to the pavement, the stopped car immediately sped away at a high rate of speed. Using his body worn radio, while maintaining a shooting position aimed at the downed subject, Chiang calls in the situation and half of the Saguaro Police Department descended upon the scene, including an air unit (copter) that began searching for the vehicle.

Investigators concluded that the deceased shooter, had not been reloading, but had been trying to clear a jam in the semi-auto AK-47 rifle he had been firing. Seasoned officers had considered it a blessing for Officer Chiang, though being the top shooter in his class, had defended himself with a handgun against an AK-47. Chiang had not felt blessed, he felt angry and so had the other 'Horsemen'. They and many others had been asking that rifles be issued to all officers since the recent uptick in violent crime. The department rejected the idea. Only members of the SWAT unit and other special enforcement teams would be assigned rifles, no one else. That was the explicit order of the Police Chief, the Mayor and City Manager. Besides, they said; "We haven't lost any officers and by all accounts, this spike in violence is only temporary." Well for David Chiang, he wasn't willing to wait, his shooting experience was too real to ignore. He overheard an old, salty patrolman who had been on the force for nearly 30 years say something to the effect that, until a cop was gunned down by the cartel, Saguaro police could kiss off the idea of arming up with rifles.

Hearing this, Chiang began to formulate a plan. What he came up with was going to be a tough sell with his Horsemen partners, but convinced it would work, he pulled them together to lay out the details and get their buy-in.

Except for Frank Garcia who was married, Kevin Galway, Marcus Johnson and David Chiang were all single men without any serious girlfriends to speak of and since this was Chiang's plan, they decided to meet at his barely furnished house to hear what he had to say. He had not minced words. Each of the Horsemen, with a cold beer in hand, listened as he boldly laid out the plan. What he had proposed was not only illegal, but reckless' dangerous in fact. Speechless, they had slowly found logic in the plan, their young cop minds spinning with 'what if' scenarios and possible pitfalls, including potentially losing their careers in law enforcement. Once set into motion, there could be no turning back.

{ CHAPTER 14 }

No going back now

Stunned, Ben Morris simply stared at a seemingly peaceful Marcus Johnson who was munching away on his turkey sub sandwich and Rainbow Snaps, like it was no big deal. The problem was a very big deal if this revelation was even close to being true and became public. If it was true, it could be one of the biggest stories to hit this city or the state for that matter.

"Marcus, that makes no sense, you're a cop, you're not a criminal, I mean you wear a badge and enforce the law, you're a man of conscious from all I can see…tell me you weren't a part of this?"

"Oh, I was though Ben, I was down with all of it."

Still unconvinced Ben responded, "So let me see if I have this straight; the four of you 'Horsemen' conspired to stage a fake cartel shooting scene, which included the shooting of one of your own in the leg so that it would demonstrate the need for the city to allow patrol officers to carry rifles on the job because a cop was attacked and shot?"

"Yeah, that's a pretty good summary of the basic plan I'd say."

Ben pushed his food forward, no longer interested in eating. After some thought, now clearly in investigative journalist mode, he asks,

"Basic plan huh? What about the details Marcus? What about those, will you tell me about them?"

Nodding his head yes, Marcus said, "I fully intend to share them, right here tonight, but are you going to finish that sandwich Ben? This confession thing has spurred an appetite like I haven't had in a very long time. Damn, we might even need some dessert! "

Dead serious and focused Ben asked, "Marcus, I suspect this plan didn't go off as you thought it would, am I correct, is that why we're really here?"

Putting his sandwich back in the rainbow-colored plastic basket, Marcus replied, "No plan goes off as expected, no matter how closely you follow the script, which we all did. On the other hand, we did so much of it right, for many years I couldn't admit what a disaster it really was from the beginning, I just wanted to believe we were doing something good. No more though, not for a long time now in fact. Let's get through this Ben while I still feel like talking and eating."

* * *

After sharing a long hard silence with disbelieving stares, the Four Horsemen, sitting in David Chiang's house in 2001, questions had erupted:

"Are you crazy?" being the first and most popular question.

"Have you thought about our careers?" being the second question most often asked.

"Where will we get the guns?"

"Who the hell is going to volunteer to be shot?"

"What will we do with the guns afterwards?"

"What role will I play?"

"Where will we all be when the fake call goes out?"

"Will I respond to the scene?"

"What if another cop shows up first?"

"What if the air unit is nearby and can light up the scene?"

"What will we tell investigators later?"

"Do we talk to each other?"

"Do we go to the hospital?"

Chiang had done his homework and had answers to their questions. The only clarification at this point had been to find the one Horseman willing to take the gunshot wound to the leg. No matter how innocuous it might be, it would hurt. In the big scheme of things, rifles for all officers to combat the enemy, it would be worth it. Although Chiang had announced that he would be the designated 'shooter", having been the acknowledged 'shooting expert' within the group, he was also willing to be the gunshot victim if needed. Chiang, in his mind, had already decided who he thought would make the perfect victim, Officer Frank Garcia.

"The guns are easy to handle, in fact I have three I'll donate to the cause." Chiang told the group. "An AK, an Uzi and a Hi-Point pistol I bought in a private sale. They're all beaters and I'm not sure I'd trust even trying to fire the Uzi. The rest we can snip off of stops; no one will miss a shooter here or there and the shitheads won't complain because they aren't supposed to be in possession to begin with."

"So, we get our feet wet becoming criminals by first stealing guns from stops? Oh cool, I can't see anything wrong with that idea." said a clearly cynical Kevin Galway.

"Wrong way to look at it dude, you're missing the bigger picture." Chiang had said, having expected this sort of reaction.

"Okay, so we get the guns and do this thing, what do we do with the guns then?" Marcus Johnson had wanted to know.

Chiang simply said, "We hide them, bury them forever, it's easy."

"Bury them where?" Marcus asked, clearly not sold on this point.

"We dig a hole nearby, but far enough from the scene to not be stumbled upon. I think in the back yard of one of the abandoned tract houses, no one would see us come or go." Chiang had answered confidently.

"David, run this through one more time now that we sort of understand the gun part, how would you envision this happening, start to finish?" Frank Garcia, who had not said a word until now, had broken his silence.

David Chiang then presented the detailed plan, from start to finish, without role names, other than noting himself as being the designated shooter:

"We decide on a good dark spot in the drop house zone, one where we can pre stage the guns. We'll have the hole dug to bury them afterwards nearby. Everyone will officially be out on patrol, but we won't call in locations. Once we're ready to go, I'll glove up and fire off a shit load of rounds, leaving casings and make it sound like the 4th of July. I then make one well aimed shot into the thigh of whoever volunteers to sustain a minor leg wound to the meaty flesh area. Collect all the guns into a bag, which one of you will drive to the hole, dropping in the bag of guns, quickly filling it in with dirt, never to be seen again. I will immediately vacate the area and when far enough away, will make a traffic stop well away from the scene. Whichever one of you is the wounded officer will hold off until we're all away from the scene, then put out an officer down and multiple shots fired call over the radio. Whoever buries the guns, and whoever else is nearby will immediately respond to the call, rendering first aid while calling for EMS, allowing more officers to respond to what will look like the scene of a huge gun battle. There will likely be 'sounds of gunfire' calls coming into dispatch from civilians, so we all have to work fast, know our role and then, follow the script. If we do that, it works."

"So that's it huh? We follow the script and it works, just like that?" Johnson had said skeptically.

"Yes, just like that." An even more confident Chiang replied.

"Alright then, let's get down to it, who's getting shot?" Galway questioned in a very serious tone.

"I mean we can vote on it. I said I'd do all the shooting part, but if no one else volunteers, I'll be the victim…and the hero of course." Chiang cleverly had offered.

"A hero….how do you get a hero out of this?" Galway had countered.

"Look at the big picture Kevin. Not only will the top brass see the need for better armed officers, but the public will see a hero cop, bravely fighting crime while being out gunned. It's inevitable." Chiang had this all figured out from start to finish.

"I'll do it." Frank Garcia volunteered, surprising everyone.

"Look, I have a wife and two kids. I'll not only be a hero in their eyes, but the Latino community will see this as a win against the cartels that are destroying everything they've been working to escape and separate themselves from. It only makes sense for it to be me. I'm the hero victim unless one of you really, really wants to get shot in the leg!" Garcia said with a big smile.

"Marcus, you bury the guns. We'll help you dig the hole before, you cool with that?" A hopeful David Chiang asked.

"I'm cool with it." Marcus replied.

"That leaves you Kevin. You'll stage north and be the first to respond, directing calls for EMS and additional officers. Chiang announced.

"I'm in, first aid and radio work." Kevin Galway said in a matter-of-fact tone.

"So, are we in agreement on the basic outline and who is going to do what?" David Chiang asked.

His fellow Horsemen had all replied in the affirmative.

The only thing left had been to execute the plan and follow the script. Something they would find out to be easier said than done.

{ CHAPTER 15 }

From plan to practice, it's show time

Three months after the meeting in David Chiang's house, officers Chiang, Johnson, Garcia, and Galway, otherwise known as the 'Four Horsemen', were ready to implement their plan, ensuring Saguaro police officers would be better armed against an increasingly violent criminal element. They had collected a cache of sacrificial rifles and pistols, all serial numbers had been removed by David Chiang, the gun guy of the group. They had dug a hole in the backyard of an abandoned house and selected an intersection further away that no longer had a working streetlight. Both locations had been in sparsely populated neighborhoods of tract homes that were known for their frequent use as drop houses, by criminals smuggling drugs and illegal aliens into the country from Mexico.

Their roles had been established; Chiang would handle all of the shooting, staging the fake cartel gun battle and the precision shot into Frank Garcia's leg. Garcia would take the hit, allowing time for everyone else to perform their part of the script. Then he would call in the emergency over the radio. After the gunfire, Marcus Johnson would quickly drive away with the bag of guns, burying them nearby in the pre-excavated hole, tossing the shovel into a nearby irrigation ditch, then head back toward the emergency call he knew would be coming. Kevin Galway, the only participant to not be present when the gunfire occurred, would be staged north of the scene, the first to respond to Garcia's calls for help over the radio. He would immediately begin to render first aid and call for more units while Chiang would be driving south and east, where once far enough away, he would attempt to make a bogus traffic stop. Once he heard Garcia's call for help, he would immediately radio dispatch, informing them he would be abandoning the traffic stop and head directly toward the emergency call, no doubt leaving behind a very confused, but relieved driver watching the red and blue lights vanish from his rear view mirror, screeching away in the opposite direction at a high rate of speed. It had come time to execute the plan, so they did.

Surprisingly, it had gone off just as planned: the fake gun battle, the precision shot to Garcia's leg; Johnson's rapid gathering of the guns into a bag, burying them in record time at the predetermined location, just as he had practiced in his mind a thousand times, prepared then to screech back to help his wounded brother. Chiang had driven almost 3 miles away and had located a vehicle to stop when, on cue, he heard the expected emergency radio call from Garcia. Galway, meanwhile, had been exactly one mile north awaiting the same call. Up to this point, everything had gone perfectly. They had all followed the script; the plan finally in action. The problem had been the emergency call from Garcia; it came out all wrong. It wasn't part of the script they had all agreed to follow. Frank Garcia's final radio call as a Saguaro police officer had been unexpected to the Horsemen; "Help me, I've been shot…I'm dying, help, please, my wife…."

* * *

Galway had not only been the first to get to Garcia as had been planned, but when he heard Garcia's pleas for help over the radio, he had raced to him faster than he had ever imagined possible; his brother was in trouble. When Galway arrived, he had come upon an unresponsive

Garcia on the ground and a tremendous amount of blood being absorbed into the sand and gravel around him. Kevin Galway had not called for help over the radio, he had screamed for it over and over! Chiang might have known his guns, but he apparently had been no expert in human anatomy; his precision gunshot had hit a major artery in Garcia's leg. With everyone focused on executing their individual role in this intricate play, no one had actually checked on Frank after he was shot, they had all just screeched off from the scene, anticipating their next part to play.

The only member of the Horsemen not at the shooting scene, by way of the plan, had been Galway. This had been his first appearance on stage and it had not been a good performance. Garcia was rapidly slipping away as Galway desperately tried to stem the flow of blood. Eventually, Galway had decided it best to simply cradle Garcia in his arms, trying to console his fallen brother, unable now to control his tears and sobs, to the point he could no longer put out radio calls.

Marcus Johnson had been next on the scene and seeing Kevin Galway holding a dying Frank Garcia, Johnson had effectively gone into shock and simply sat down on the ground beside them both, not making any radio calls for help. In fact, he made no sound at all.

{ CHAPTER 16 }

All cards and Rainbow Snaps are on the table

Ben Morris simply stares at Marcus Johnson, not saying a word. Johnson had finished his and Ben's turkey club sandwiches, and only the Rainbow Snaps that came with Ben's meal remain uneaten.

"Frank Garcia? Did he…is he dead?" Ben asked, in a voice barely louder than a hoarse whisper.

"He died Ben. EMS and Fire got there fast actually, so did Chiang who was running around with bandages and attempting CPR, but he was wasting his time. Frank died in Kevin's arms, and I was sitting there powerless to do anything about it. I was frozen, just paralyzed." Marcus admitted.

Then looking like he was in some faraway place, Marcus continued without any prompting from Ben, as though Marcus wasn't really speaking to him, but to a different audience. Regardless, he just sat and listened, without interruption, to the uncomfortable story, like a priest during confession.

"It was a nightmare. We wanted to go in the ambulance or at least follow it to the hospital even though we knew Frank was gone, we needed to be with our brother, and they wouldn't let us. The investigators were showing up hard and fast, we had to answer questions, walk through it all over and over again a thousand fucking times! GOD DAMN IT, I'm done talking, I need to get to my brother. Christ I seriously thought about curb stomping one particular prick detective that didn't even seem to recognize the fact a cop was dead; my friend was dead. But no, big detective asshole was questioning me about Frank like we were talking about some shithead from the street being popped, not one of us, the good guys, you know? Shit man, I could have shot that prick and realize now I was seriously thinking about it in my head because I was so far gone at that time.

"They separated us; we couldn't talk to each other, me Chiang and Galway, so we stuck to the script and as crazy as it sounds now, they bought it. It was 5 days later before the three of us thought it safe enough to actually discuss what happened and we of course agreed that all we had to do now was ride it out. None of us even realized what that could possibly mean. We had all individually and together met with Frank's wife and two young kids, who I avoid today when I can because I can't face knowing how I was a part of them losing their husband and father. The local media of course picked up the story and for a short time it went national; Brave young Latino cop stands up to a violent, heavily armed criminal cartel. He was a hero before he went into the ground and the hardest part was that all of us, me, David, and Kevin, we had to be a part of it because the story of the Four Horsemen was out. I wanted to go to another country on the other side of the planet, find a deep hole, climb in, and never come out again. It was the worst time of my life.

"The stupid, insane plan was working, and we had lost a brother because of it, but couldn't tell anyone. Except for repeated questioning by investigators and some grumblings, rumors of a sort about something being fishy with the story, it blew over. Not only was Frank Garcia a hero, dead as he was, the City Council immediately heard complaints from constituents calling for an end to these heavily armed thugs and wondering why a brave hero like Officer Francisco Garcia wasn't armed with at least a rifle? Eight months after the time of Frank's death, the department had initially developed a rifle qualification program for any officers who were willing to buy their own rifle, but quickly that was squelched when the city miraculously found dollars from the Parks and Recreation budget that would buy the rifles for patrol officers willing and able to pass the qualification process.

"The funeral was brutal. David, Kevin, and I were expected to get up and speak because everyone in the department and viewers of television news and newspapers back then understood, we were brothers. We kept it together as best we could, but Galway couldn't finish his prepared words and we pulled him back away from the microphone while the Catholic priest consoled him. David and I did the best we could, but with the lights, not being able to see the audience inside, knowing what we said was being broadcast on a live feed, we kept it pretty close to our chest, but made it known Frank Garcia was a true hero, willing to sacrifice his life for the city he loved. At the suggestion of the department, we all took 2 weeks off, instructed to not clock in vacation hours on a time sheet; our absence was being covered by precinct timekeepers. Given the time off, the three of us met and finally talked about what went down. We agreed to just keep on working and let it all die down, so we did.

"It was weird, guys looked at us different and began to put more distance between them and us. We didn't know if it was them suspecting something or just providing space to grieve? It didn't matter, we initially went out and played it plain vanilla; taking calls as they came, but not aggressively looking for criminals and that's what we did for a couple of months without incident. About 3 months after, David began to change, he seemed to be avoiding me and Kevin, seeming to not respond to calls he knew we were involved with. Not only that, but he also got popped by Internal Affairs for an 'excessive use of force' charge. Word in the locker room was he went off on some Hispanic kid that really wasn't doing anything wrong other than having tinted windows. This wasn't David's sort of thing, he was always cool with kids, especially minority kids like he had once been. It was the first red flag.

"A month later he was assisting on a call with an already cuffed perp. David punched him, which is a huge NO-NO! He was suspended without pay for two weeks, a serious punishment, just short of termination. He stopped talking to me and Kevin on the job except for pre-shift roll call and that was only when the Sergeant asked us all direct questions about some call we had all responded to. He was avoiding us. We both tried to call him off duty and he wouldn't take our calls, he was clearly unraveling, but was dead set on not letting us help.

"Then, almost six months after Frank died, David was involved in an off duty 'road rage' situation, brandished a gun, threatened to kill the guy he perceived to have cut him off in traffic. Well, the city had had enough, they were seriously considering the idea of having the County Attorney bring him up on criminal charges, the city wasn't going to back officer Chiang on this; he'd gone too far. Then to the surprise of everyone, David resigned from the police department, turned in his badge and city issued sidearm. He was done and didn't care about any possible County prosecution charges. Because he had isolated himself so much, Kevin and I didn't even know about all this until two days later and only because it came from our squad Sergeant. We tried to call, but as I said before, David had stopped taking our calls at that point, at least two or three months prior. Kevin and I agreed to go to David's house on our next day off, which was only three days away. We figured we'd talk to him, convince him to reconsider, talk about what he was dealing with, talk it out with his brothers, just help him figure it out, you know? We did just that. The problem was that David Chiang had moved out; the house was empty with a For Sale realty sign posted in front. We were stunned.

"It doesn't take an experienced cop to know that if you want answers, you ask questions, which is what we did to a curious senior citizen woman in the next yard looking at us closely. She asked if we knew David and we said we worked with him. She told us he moved to Colorado to live with his older brother. He apparently had an older brother by one year, but, because they looked so much alike, people assumed they were twins. Although this was news to both Kevin and I, this woman was a fount of information, in fact she was still yapping as we drove away! I got to say it was embarrassing realizing a complete stranger knew more personal details about one of our closest friends than we did. Life seemed to offer only difficult surprises in those days.

"For all intents and purposes, David dropped off the face of the earth as far as Saguaro PD was concerned. Then about two months later, he seemed to literally drop off the face of the earth for everyone when a local law enforcement agency in Colorado fielded a missing person's report for David and his brother Joseph. They hadn't been seen or heard from for almost two weeks by the time a concerned family member from California called local Colorado authorities with concerns. Colorado then contacted Saguaro PD after running David's information through their computer systems. According to what we heard in the precinct, Colorado police had no idea where they might be, only able to say the home they lived in showed no signs of foul play or criminal activity, although the older brother Joseph's Toyota 4-Runner was missing, but Chiang's Ford F-150 was parked safely inside the garage, it was a mystery, but nothing to dwell on for Saguaro PD.

"For me and Kevin, it was different. We did dwell on it; we dwelt on it a lot in fact, because if Chiang decided to tell his story, we were toast. All we could do was work and wait, which we did."

{ CHAPTER 17 }

Clarity leads to more confusion

"So I assume David Chiang never revealed the truth about what actually happened?" Ben Morris asked, slowly regaining his footing after a mind blowing listening session.

"I don't know. If he did, that person has never come forward. After so many years I lost any concern I ever had of it happening, especially since I know David won't be telling the story." Marcus Johnson responded.

"I take it then, that David Chiang is dead?"

"Yes, a long time ago in fact, but like everything else in this fucked up affair, his death was weird." Marcus admitted.

"What do you mean weird? I thought he was a missing person… when was he found, when did he die?" Ben asked excitedly.

"Okay, there's more to say about Chiang. Then I got something else to tell you, so sit back and listen. Ask your girlfriend to bring us some coffee and one of those glazed muffins. I need something sweet to eat." With that, Marcus continued to tell Ben about the mysterious demise of David Chiang, followed by more recent concerns.

* * *

"It was probably a year or 14 months after David quit the force when we got the news. I had already changed squads in the precinct, I was on days then and Kevin (Galway) was still on second shift, so we rarely, if ever saw each other on the job. Frankly, we hardly saw each other off the job either, but still talked by phone once in a while. The news came down to us through the precinct that the bodies of brothers David and Joseph Chiang had been discovered by a hiker in a very remote area of Colorado. The location of the bodies was more than two hundred miles from Joseph's home that he had shared with David. From what local investigators could determine, Joseph had been shot in the head, but due to the condition of the remaining bones caused by weather and obvious animal scavengers, it's unclear if he had been shot by someone or had committed an act of suicide. The ballistics indicated the round used came from a 9mm firearm, which was never recovered. A very short distance away, the body of David Chiang was found hanging from a high branch in a tree. Animals had not been able to ravage his body except for squirrels, which didn't do enough damage to prevent an autopsy, although decomposition was advanced due to having endured a full year's weather cycle.

"Although not impossible, a random double murderer at work was not the theory local investigators were pursuing, but more that of a murder/suicide situation. In either case, it was baffling; no known motive, no message left behind, Joseph's vehicle was still missing. There were no known financial or family troubles. No firearm was ever recovered. The mysterious deaths were entered into in the 'cold case' file, likely to never be resolved.

"It was enough though, that Kevin and I connected via phone, we agreed to meet and discuss the news. We met at a bar for a beer, sat off to ourselves in a booth, while a pool tournament was going on, no one even noticed us. We both agreed that David had gone bat shit crazy and for some reason killed his brother, then himself. Nothing we could do about that, but we had to wonder if David had told his brother or anyone else about what really happened to Frank Garcia. We agreed it'd be best if we played it cool about the news of David, don't do anything to draw attention to either of us, just go on and work. I told Kevin I was planning to drop paper for a different precinct north of Southern Vista and he thought it might be a good idea. He wished me good luck. Two months later I was on a day patrol in part of the city so unlike what I was used to, I sometimes didn't know where I was....there was literally no crime! I rapidly came to like it; no shitheads, no gangs, no gunfire, no graffiti, no Four Horsemen references. It was paradise for a cop wanting to fly under the radar."

* * *

"So that was the way life went for the next 20 years Ben. Galway stayed down south until he successfully tested for Sergeant, about the time your news report implicated him and several other officers in an overtime payment scam, which he wasn't guilty of, by the way. I know. I did some snooping. I continued to move to other places where I could basically hide from the street, I'd had my fill of the street. I wore the badge and still do today, but I can't look in the mirror and see a cop. I haven't been able to for many years in fact. I'm an imposter, Ben, just hiding from my sins." A contrite Marcus Johnson admitted.

"I'm not going to argue the case for or against Galway and the overtime thing, I'm sure you had information that said otherwise, that's not what we're here about. You told me about David Chiang, but you said you had something else, what is it?" Ben asked seriously.

"This past April the bag of guns I buried back in 2001 was found." Marcus simply said.

"The same guns from the scheme you guys concocted and participated in that killed Frank Garcia?" Ben asked in a hushed tone.

"Yes, those guns. Galway called and told me about it when it happened. It was a fluke they were even found, some guy wanting to plant a tree, or something like that, purely an accident. Shit, even Kevin finding out about it was by accident since he's got his own squad up north now. Well, you know what I mean." Marcus said and went silent.

"What are the implications? Will they find fingerprints or DNA?

Does the department know you and Galway were involved?" a flustered Ben asked, so full of questions that suddenly it was hard to remain calm.

Sensing this, Marcus soothingly said, "Hey man, slow your ride down. If they know anything, they haven't showed their hand and it's been what, like 5 months? They may very well know, and I suspect that if they do, they're figuring how to play it, especially with Kevin's situation, which brings us to here and now my friend. Speaking of that Ben, are we friends?"

Ben sighed, "Full disclosure Marcus, any friend from my past never dropped a shit bomb in my lap like you have. But yes, we're friends. In fact, I might be the only friend you have right now."

Ben continued as Marcus listened, "We need to know more about how and why Kevin Galway died. We also need to know about the status of those guns, are they connected?"

"Well, I'm going to Kevin's funeral on Thursday, although I won't be asking questions, I'll be keeping my ear to the ground and see what I can pick up from the other cops. I know right now they think he popped himself and made it look like a murder. It makes sense so his wife can collect on the benefits. Yeah, I can do that easy enough, but there's no way I can ask anything about those guns. I might as well be confessing to the whole thing if I did that." Marcus stated plainly.

"Okay, you do that, and I have a long shot idea about the guns, but damn man, this is nuts and getting crazier by the minute. I don't even have a damned cell phone Marcus; how do I reach you?" an extremely frustrated Ben declared.

"Thought you'd never ask, Friend." said a smiling Marcus as he handed over a cell phone to Ben.

"A burner phone dude, you're paid up for 90 days, just don't waste the minutes on 'sex calls'."

"I'll let you know if I get any vibes or info at the funeral about Kevin's case, but I don't think it will be much if anything. I'm more interested in the guns, so let me know what you have up your sleeve, run it by me first before getting yourself in too deep, something you aren't able to handle." Marcus was sincere in his concern for dragging Ben into this mess.

"Absolutely, I'll know more on Thursday, and we can take it from there." Ben told Marcus, matter-of-factly. Silently he was far from confident that he'd be able to find an avenue leading to information. In fact, Ben found tremendous irony that on Thursday, Marcus would be attending a funeral, while Ben might also be planning a funeral for his own career, a career clinging to life support.

{ CHAPTER 18 }

Saguaro PD Crime Lab, Main Police Headquarters

It had been nearly two weeks since senior lab technician Bill Winters had been instructed to conduct a ballistics test on the rifle found with David Chiang's fingerprint. This test had been conducted by the team with results provided to Bill. What the team had not known was the discreet other instruction given to Bill by his superior; review old records related to the ballistics report of a projectile found in the leg of a deceased officer killed in the line of duty, Officer Frank Garcia. Bill had reviewed the data and now needed to report the results to his supervisor, Sergeant Vernon 'Vern' Kerley. This should be interesting.

Without calling ahead, Bill exited the environmentally controlled area of the crime lab, walking directly into the administrative area of work cubicles, and the only walled office, that of Sergeant Kerley, the man he needed to talk to. The door to the office was open, and Vern, reading glasses on, was closely studying some papers in an open file on his desk. Bill knocked on the door frame, and announced himself. Sergeant Kerley motioned him in, telling him to shut the door behind him, which he did, immediately sitting in one of two chairs in front of the Sergeant's desk.

"Although I oversee you tech geeks, day in and day out, you realize I'm still a cop, right Bill?" Bill simply nodded in agreement, as Vern continued, "Good, because I can tell from looking at you that what you're about to tell me isn't going to be news I'll be happy to hear, right, Bill?"

Bill Winters, with his best poker face said, "Sergeant, I don't know if you'll like it or not. I'm simply here to give you the data you requested, that's all."

"Yeah, fair enough Bill, I shouldn't have pulled that old cop shit on you of all people. So, tell me what you found."

"Well, I don't know if it was a hunch, or what that you had, but the projectile recovered from the leg of Officer Frank Garcia matched exactly to a test round fired from the AK-47 with a fingerprint discovered on a partially loaded magazine that belonged to a deceased former police officer, that being David Chiang. That's the report I have for you Sergeant."

"Who else knows this?" Kerley asked directly.

"Well, the forensic team for one. They of course, know the results of the ballistics test, which obviously came from the same rifle that had David Chiang's fingerprint. That in itself, well, that's simply data, nothing more."

"Does anyone else know about the match to the Garcia bullet?"

"No. The only two people that know that are you and me." Bill now sat wondering what would come next, wanting Sergeant Kerley to shed light upon this mystery. To his disappointment, the Sergeant went full cop on him, which he knew was likely, but had hoped he might be afforded more professional courtesy.

"Okay, Bill, that's what I needed to know. Thank you for the information, you and your team are the very best, keep up the good work. The City of Saguaro appreciates all you do!"

"Oh wait, Bill one more thing, do you have anything new on this north side rapist?"

"No, sorry, Sarge, but Jenkins is working hard on it, he hasn't stopped since we last talked to you in fact.

"Oh yes, Randall Jenkins, good Christ." Vern muttered while loudly sighing.

Bill quickly countered, "Look, Sergeant, I know he's not your favorite sort, but he really is good at what he does. In fact he's probably the most dedicated person I have on the team."

"Look I know, I know, I really do. It's just that for some reason he gets under my skin. It's not just him, but it seems like all of these young people today come from a different planet than the one I've always lived on." Vern Kerley admitted, clearly disappointed he had said anything at all.

"Sergeant, I completely understand what you're saying, I see it too, but I'm working closely with these younger folks every day, so I suppose I've become a bit more immune to the difference in culture." A sincere Bill said in a soothing manner.

"I hear you Bill. I'm not keeping up with the times, I realize it. This isn't public knowledge, but I'm seriously looking at retirement. I'm not sure I'm up for all the BS and red tape anymore. One more policy change or public relations overhaul and I'm calling it."

Bill listened respectfully before speaking, "Well Sergeant, we wouldn't want to see you go, but I can understand your reasoning."

"Alright, let's get back to work and hey Bill, I wasn't blowing smoke earlier, your team really is the best and the city does appreciate all you do. Listen, don't mention anything to Jenkins about what I said, that wasn't right. In fact, tell him I mentioned him by name in a positive way, make something up."

These were Sergeant Kerley's words to Senior Civilian Lab Technician Bill Winters as he left the office. Now Vern had to get his presentation together for the meeting with his own boss, which could be dicey.

{ CHAPTER 19 }

Probation Headquarters,
Saguaro, Arizona, August 2020

"Are you fucking crazy Morris? You want me to what? Just because you got some fucking, wait, let me look at my notes. You're selling fucking donuts and coffee in the shithead park on Saturdays, and you want me to jeopardize my career asking about some fucking rusty guns that supposedly were dug up? Hey, man, you might be but I'm not crazy, so FUCK NO!"

Not finished, an animated Probation Officer Julio Chavez continued on. "You come in here with some crazy story you have that will make you bigger than 'Woodward and Bernstein', won't tell me shit about it, but expect me to go around asking about some rusty guns? Give me a fucking break man. I could violate you right now, just on that suggestion alone, you'll be back on a metal cot in County before the sun sets."

Fully expecting exactly such a reception, Ben Morris calmly said, "Yes, you could, but you won't, because you need something. Not just answers to your questions about how Kevin Galway died, but more than that, I suspect. If this story blows, it helps you Officer Chavez."

A now more subdued, and again seated Chavez slowly breathed, allowing what he just heard to settle in. Finally he asked, "Helps me how?"

"Look, I can't give you the details, but when this story breaks, and it will, you'll be seen to be a hero in how it goes down, likely assuring you at least a promotion, maybe even a bigger opportunity for your career." Morris soothingly said.

"Let's be straight Morris, I don't like you, I don't trust you and as far as I'm concerned, I've got all I need to send your sorry ass back to the tank. I can deny absolutely everything we've talked about, and I know you don't have the ability to record shit right now. Say I do some poking around? Where do we go from there? I mean if there is even a there, there? Fuck, you got me talking like an idiot now. You know what I mean Morris, what's next?"

"Just call me, I have a cell phone now, which I need to officially record in your Probationary record of me, PO1058 is what my legal papers say I'm being tracked as." Ben said this while holding back a smile.

"A cell phone, you been holding out on me Morris? That doesn't help your case, you know. Wait a minute, you been tapping that fat dyke of a boss, trying to turn her? Good luck with that shit. From what I know she's a hard core 'pussy only' sort when it comes to sex, but if it gets you free coffee and a cell phone, I won't criticize." A snarky sounding Julio Chavez said.

"No, it didn't come from Shelley. The phone came from my source. He's serious about this story, a story that might show you in a good light. More than that, it's very helpful since I have several irons in the fire right now, a big story like this. Oh, dang it, I didn't realize this phone had audio recording capability, imagine that?" Ben added smugly.

Except that Ben was anything but smug after he left his meeting. He didn't know exactly what he should do next. Had he just earned himself a ticket back to jail? First things first; get over to "Bathsheba's Rainbow Bistro" ASAP! He was already missing work, something he desperately needed in order to eat.

{ CHAPTER 20 }

Saguaro PD Main Precinct building

Sergeant Vernon 'Vern' Kerley was heading to the office of his boss, Lieutenant Larry Osco. Larry was an old PD veteran that had worked with Vern, back when they were young patrolmen, in an ugly section within the north part of Saguaro that had not received the same amount of media attention as the southern parts of the city. However, the area they worked had been infamous for the occasional crazy violent events that sold newspapers and drove television ratings. Still, because these outbreaks of violent crime had been so sporadic, the focus had always been down south. The area in question had essentially been owned and terrorized by violent, outlaw motorcycle clubs (gangs) that were continuously battling for control of the area, the city and the county. Eventually, a notorious national motorcycle club had won the territory, declaring it to be their turf, and still does to this day, drawing little to no media attention.

Lt. Osco was hoping beyond hope that the reason for this meeting was because Kerley had evidence to arrest and convict this 'North-side Serial Rapist', a piece of shit that not only needed to be shot on sight, but instead was destroying the reputation of the Saguaro Police Department by way of local media. It would not be long before national 'cop hating' networks decided to involve themselves into the mix. The situation needed to be resolved quickly, but that wasn't the news Lt. Osco would receive from his old friend, now subordinate, Vern Kerley.

"What do you have Vern? I hope it's good because I have the Chief breathing down my neck. Please make me a happy man today." Lt. Osco offered hopefully.

Cautiously, Vern spoke, "Lieutenant, I'm going to shut the door." He closed the door and sat in a chair. "What I have isn't good news at all in my view. In fact it's off the charts crazy. In fact, I'm not exactly sure how to say it." Vern Kerley did say it though, all of it.

Arms firmly crossed, Lt. Osco wasn't happy with how the direction the meeting had taken by way of Vern's report.

"For the love of all things holy Vern, you're telling me that fucking dead lunatic David Chiang, he killed his partner too?" Lt. Osco was visibly furious. He leaned over the desk and snarled at Kerley, purposely not raising his voice.

Sergeant Kerley was quick to respond, "That's not what I'm saying at all. What the lab has determined was that a buried rifle, discovered last April, with David Chiang's fingerprint discovered on an inserted, partially loaded magazine, was the same rifle used to fire a projectile that matched the bullet removed from the leg of fallen officer, Frank Garcia." Pausing, "Beyond those data points, I'm not suggesting anything, I'm just telling you something I think you need to know and asking how you want me to handle it going forward. No one, except for the Senior Civilian Lab Tech knows the connection between the rifle and Garcia. He can be trusted to not share that information." Vern remained silent, in his chair, waiting for whatever fury might come his way.

"I remember talking to my dad back in Arkansas when I would call him on the phone every Sunday afternoon. I was thinking about taking the test for Sergeant at the time. Jesus, that was years back in the day Vern, it seems forever ago now. He told me to do it, but only if I understood that it would mean I'd be accepting responsibility for men below me, no matter their actions. No matter what it was, their actions would put my ass on the line. I wish for once my dad hadn't been right". Lt. Osco stated, sitting back in his chair.

Vern, hoping to help, quickly offered, "Well Larry, I'm sorry sir, I mean Lieutenant. Neither Chiang nor Garcia worked for you. I wouldn't take this personal. I mean, whatever the situation was, it shouldn't reflect on you, you're just the keeper and finder of new data."

After a very long pause, Lt. Osco simply responded, "You know it doesn't work that way Vern, shit rolls downhill fast, like lava from a Hawaiian volcano, all while tourists snap pictures. The only way this comes out is if we have answers to how and why this 'data' exists. Do you have any theories? If so, hit me with them, because I'm struggling right now."

"Actually, I do, but you won't like it and neither will the heads of the department." Vern quickly offered.

"Fuck the department, tell me what you think this shit might mean, I'll deal with the department later, I want to know now what you're on to." Osco said desperately.

* * *

Kerley laid out the theory he had formed, starting from the minute Bill Winters and Randall Jenkins delivered the news about the fingerprint found on the magazine of the AK-47 rifle that had been accidentally discovered in the backyard of a South Saguaro home. When Bill Winters confirmed that the AK-47 rifle tied to David Chiang was the same rifle that shot hero officer Frank Garcia, his theory became more solid as to what had transpired. Lt. Larry Osco took it all in and after many minutes of reflection, he offered a summary of what he had just heard, including the theory presented by his old friend.

"Okay, I think I have it now." This was Lieutenant Osco feeding back the theory to Sergeant Kerley. "You think that fucking loony Chiang stole the truck with all the guns awaiting transport to the armory? Okay, I can see that, although I think he'd have paid someone else to do it. No matter, he apparently was a gun nut, everyone said that. Then, Frank Garcia, a squad mate, figures it out, tells Chiang he knows and wants to meet with him to persuade him into what, confessing? If so, I'm not buying into that part."

Without waiting for a response from Kerley, Osco continued, "Weren't Chiang and Garcia tight, along with some others? What the hell did they call themselves, the "Justice League" or some stupid shit like that, right? Okay, let's forget that for now, Garcia and Chiang meet, Chiang shoots him with a stolen rifle, then uses more of those stolen guns to blast off hundreds of rounds, making it look like a cartel gunfight that Garcia gets caught up in. Chiang then buries the guns. I'm following you up to that point, but how do you explain Garcia's radio calls for help? Why shoot him in the leg and not the heart or head if he wanted to kill him?"

"I'm not sure why, maybe he was just trying to intimidate him, you know, show him he was serious?" Vern offered weakly.

"Look, I know it's just a theory, and I asked to hear it, but it just doesn't add up Vern." The Lieutenant said and continued on, "I can completely buy into Chiang stealing those guns based on his later behavior, but we have no proof of that. Hell, the fingerprint could have come from a legitimate stop he had made. The confiscated rifle could have been sitting in local storage, to await transport, along with the others well before the whole load was stolen. Those stolen guns could have found their way back into cartel hands and that rifle was the one used to shoot Garcia. I mean, if Chiang was alive and on trial, that's what his defense lawyer would be telling a jury."

Vern had always considered himself to be a good street cop and detective, but he realized now how good Larry Osco had been too; these were details Vern hadn't considered until just now.

"Damn Lieutenant, I hadn't thought about that possibility, I just for some reason jumped on Chiang being dirty for this." Vern sheepishly admitted.

"Don't think what I just said to be fact Vern. Chiang was clearly crazy, we know that now, but crazy doesn't have to mean dirty. Your theory could well be right, but I'm not of a mind to throw this skunk on the desk of the Chief. That would be suicide right now." Lt. Osco stated firmly.

"What do you want me to do with this information?"

"Bury it. If anyone asks about prints, we offer only that a fingerprint of a long dead officer was found and believe it to have been left years earlier during a legitimate traffic stop and arrest. That rifle is suspected to have been part of a larger group of legally confiscated firearms that while awaiting transport to the armory for further disposition, were all stolen. Although unsolved, investigators then and now believe the firearms were stolen by Mexican Cartel members operating at the time in the Southern Vista Precinct area. The cache of firearms found buried in the backyard of an unsuspecting young family, were likely placed there at an earlier time by cartel operatives for unknown reasons." Lieutenant Osco laid out the makings of a potential future statement released to the media.

"So, no mention of Garcia at all?" asked Vern.

"Not one word. He's a hero, we keep it that way."

"Yes sir."

"One more thing Vern, this civilian, Winters? You say he's solid and will keep quiet?" Lt. Osco asked with a hint of concern in his voice.

"Lieutenant, rest easy. The information is safe with him. I'd bet my badge on it"

{ CHAPTER 21 }

Cop funerals; hard for everyone except who's being buried

It was a sad day for those who support law enforcement, especially in and around Saguaro, Arizona. Representatives from agencies all over the state attended the funeral of Sergeant Kevin Galway. Family, friends, and countless fellow officers were there, struggling in grief, and tightly packed into the large church. This somber event was different from others in an unspoken way, not readily noticed by the public. Because of the circumstances surrounding his death, the aura present was different than in funerals for other fallen officers as the audience was not in agreement as to his demise.

Family and close friends that weren't cops were convinced that Kevin had been murdered. Most of his fellow officers were equally certain Galway committed suicide; having attempted to stage the scene to look like a homicide, likely to ensure his wife would receive his death benefits. Neither side was going to debate topic, at least not at the funeral, so the resultant mood was terribly sad and restrained.

City leaders, including the Chief of Police, avoided the details of the tragic loss when speaking at the funeral. Through the numerous prayers, touching music selections and a well-produced, heart wrenching slide show, which depicted Kevin advancing in life from a toddler to a smiling, recently promoted Sergeant of the Saguaro PD, Marcus Johnson sat heart broken in silence.

Silent, but listening intently like never before; he heard hushed comments, smirks and even cursing. Cops typically appear stoic in these events, but they're quietly venting amongst themselves, something the public never sees' or would understand. He heard what he expected; the cops think Kevin popped himself, no doubt about it. He didn't hear a peep about the discovery of the buried guns though, so he hoped that Ben Morris had something up his sleeve. If not, Marcus was finished, at least in his mind. He was of the belief that police investigators and the County Attorney were currently making a case against him, the lone 'Horseman' as he silently grieved the loss of not just Kevin Galway, but for Frank Garcia and David Chiang as well.

The only comforting thought he had was that when his funeral came, possibly soon, he wouldn't be joining those in grief. His funeral would mark his freedom from the poisonous burden eating him away, more and more each passing day.

{ CHAPTER 22 }

Probationary benefits

It had been nearly a week since Probation Officer Julio Chavez met with case number "PO1958", more commonly known as, fallen from grace, local newspaper and television investigative reporter, Ben Morris, currently on probation in the County of Hohokam, Arizona. Chavez harbors a sincere dislike for Ben personally, thinking him to be a privileged 'pretty boy' that never paid his dues in life. Even after Ben had been found guilty of drug possession, served six months in the county jail, lost his job and ability to restart his career and is now residing in a flop house; Julio Chavez still had no sympathy for him.

However, Chavez conceded that when Ben had been working, at least on television, he had delivered some hard-hitting reports. As such, he secretly respected the skill set that his charge possessed. More importantly sees it now as a way to advance his own career in the Probation Office bureaucracy. Chavez had been thinking about it and decided to call someone from his vast digital rolodex.

"Bill Winters, not sure you remember me, Julio Chavez, I'm your brother's Probation Officer. We've spoken a few times in the past about his case and progression."

Stunned Bill answered, "Well yes Officer Chavez, I do remember you. I'm hoping nothing is wrong. I haven't heard from my brother in a couple of weeks. Is everything okay?"

"No, no, no, it's not like he's in the hospital or anything like that, well, at least that I know of. I have some concerns from local police, issues I see as possibly affecting the conditions of his probationary terms." Chavez said in a matter-of-fact way.

"Damn it, he's been doing great, I can't believe he's screwing up now. What did he do?" Bill asked frantically.

"Calm down, I'm not sure of anything. Because of the information, I'd rather not discuss it over the phone. Can you meet me for coffee?"

* * *

"No, I don't know anything. Even if I did, I wouldn't divulge it to you or to anyone. I'm sworn to secrecy to protect private and criminal cases and you of all people should know that." An indignant Bill Winters told Julio Chavez in a coffee and donut shop that has been in business since the early 50's.

"Wow, thanks for the ethics lesson Bill. Consider me to be officially chastised. However, you didn't allow me a chance to expand on why I'm even asking."

"Well, no I didn't. I just can't see what this has to do with my brother, what am I missing?" Bill replied, clearly frustrated at this point.

"It might not have anything to do with him at all. If it plays out how I think it will, it might only be in a very indirect way, but I need to find out for sure. The fact is I have another, 'client' that says your brother shared information with him in jail related to the recent death of a police officer, Sergeant Kevin Galway. It might lead to information confirming that he was in fact murdered and didn't commit suicide as has been suggested, an ugly accusation in my opinion." Chavez said soothingly.

"All right, I mean, I'm not exactly tracking here…this is surprising news, but Junior has always been, well always close to trouble. I'm sure you know that by seeing his file." Bill replied.

Chavez pounced quickly, "Oh hey, I think he's a good guy, just misunderstood. He sort of reminds me of many guys I served with in the Army, a bit crazy, but cool. No Bill, I feel comfortable with him, I'm here to help him in fact, that's my job. I can't help him though without some information; I need to find out if this other guy I'm dealing with is feeding me a load of shit or if there's trouble with your brother's case, that's why I came to you. What do you know about the death of Sergeant Kevin Galway and that of a bag of guns that were discovered in April in south Saguaro?"

Never failing to cover for his older brother since childhood, Bill had always looked up to him. Yet, his older brother had consistently let him down, always doing the wrong thing. His brother was clearly the 'black sheep' of the family. Regardless, Bill Winters had never given up hope for him to get 'right' in life. Thus Bill confided to Julio that he knew nothing related to the death of Sergeant Galway, but he did know about the buried bag of guns: the confirmed rifle fingerprint, the ballistic results from the rifle, including the old ballistics report of the bullet recovered from the leg of a fallen hero, Officer Frank Garcia.

Although Bill was still wondering how his older brother could have been made privy to this specific controversy, he realized that if he didn't cooperate now, his brother might go back to jail or possibly prison. This was simply not something he could accept. He did know Julio Chavez had him over a barrel and he no longer had a hand to play, he was committed now.

Julio on the other hand was elated now that he had information he could use. His problem was exactly how to use it. His best and only avenue being that of the 'client' he hated most, Ben Morris. It might be time to cooperate, which was fine, as long as he came out on top.

{ CHAPTER 23 }

Comparing notes and making plans

Ben Morris received a call on the burner phone that Marcus Johnson had provided him. The call wasn't from Marcus, but from his Probation Officer Julio Chavez, who wanted to meet. Chavez didn't want to meet in his office and Ben didn't want him anywhere near "Bathsheba's Rainbow Bistro, so they agreed to meet at the downtown public library. Finally, they made their way past the hordes of homeless people that use the library as a place to squat during operating hours. The city had been unable to legally remove them, so they've become an unsavory fixture. Chavez told Ben what he found out about the case of Kevin Galway, which amounted to nothing. As for the buried guns, that information was much more interesting to hear about. Chavez of course, wouldn't reveal his source, seemingly concerned only with how this information might make him a celebrated public servant, fostering a serious advance to his career.

Ben, playing his cards close to his chest, revealed only that he was sat atop a huge story that he was arranging to release through local media. Not only would the story be the biggest thing since the shootout at the O.K. Corral, it would also mark Ben's return as a top notch investigative reporter. He will credit Julio and his successful efforts at reforming persons on probation into productive citizens once again. Skeptical, but figuring he had nothing to lose, Chavez accepted Ben's game plan, with the caveat he be kept informed. He also reminded Ben that their weekly meetings would be a good time for updates on the breaking news story. With no further need of the public library, or the homeless throng, Ben and Julio went their separate ways.

* * *

"How the hell can you afford a cell phone? It can't be from the peanuts I'm paying you!" The gruff voice of Shelley Conner said into her phone after receiving an unexpected call.

"I got it from my buddy, the one you let me meet with at the shop. He's helping me out." Ben Morris said to his boss and owner of Bathsheba's Rainbow Bistro.

"Oh, I'm sure he's helping all right, I don't want to even begin to imagine how you're helping him, but I'm not here to judge anyone, otherwise God will strike me dead, she's a real bitch you know?" Shelley said in a snarky tone.

"Look Shelley, I told you it's not like that, but...okay, hey it doesn't matter, he is helping me and I'm trying to help him. Can he and I meet again at the shop, we need to discuss some important things and he really seems to like the food and drinks."

"Sure, I don't see any harm, but I hope you guys are paying, this shit ain't free handsome. Not for you or your special friend, you understand?" A stern Shelley Conner replied.

"Thanks Shelley and no worries about the paying thing, we even tip well." Ben said, smiling to himself as he planned the next phone call he had to make.

* * *

"Hey Marcus, it's Ben, I was wondering if we could meet up and compare notes, I have some information you'll want to hear and I'm wondering what you found out at the funeral, you think you can do that?" This message Ben left on Marcus's voice mailbox. Marcus was likely on duty as a police resource officer at a central city elementary school.

Ben sat back in the barely furnished room at the Del Vista West building, his current home, which, in his view, was a very small step up from a county jail cell. He wasn't scheduled to work today, normally a bad thing, but right now he needed time to reflect about many things; Marcus's mental and emotional state, this crazy story line, Ben's own current life and, future, if there is one, Julio Chavez and his evil plotting, and too many ugly things in between.

One burning issue to consider was how and why Kevin Galway, now having been laid to rest with full honors, had died. Had he killed himself or had he been murdered? If he had killed himself, had it been because of a story Ben broke a couple of years back, revealing a group of police officers that had been working off duty for a shady security company, a company owned by the local owner and operator of a string of Saguaro area pawn shops, known to traffic in stolen merchandise? The off duty jobs were legal in and of themselves, as many police officers supplemented their limited incomes. The problem was that some officers, perhaps not all, were also fraudulently reporting overtime on their City of Saguaro time sheets, for the same hours they were working on the supplemental jobs.

It had been a big story and had gained Ben Morris a spot in the bright lights of Arizona media for a few weeks with his highly anticipated follow-up reporting. Although it had resulted in some very terse and embarrassed statements from the Saguaro Chief of Police and subordinates over those weeks, it ended up producing more smoke than actual fire, but the damage had been done. Kevin Galway had been one of the names on the list of police officers involved. Had he killed himself out of shame, although his death came well after the story and disciplinary actions handed out by the police department? Despite the story, Galway had been selected and promoted to the rank of Sergeant. Suicide for that reason just didn't make sense to Ben.

What about murder? When Galway died, Ben had no longer been employed in the media industry. In fact, he had been close to homelessness or back in jail, until landing the part time job at a coffee bistro in the art district. His former news colleagues were running with the shady cause of death story, going so far as to suggest Galway had been about to provide details related to the shady owner of the pawn shops and security company, a man that had often been linked to criminal activity, with rumored connections to Mexican Cartel money.

Had the pawn shop owner or Cartel silenced Galway? Marcus told Ben that Galway, although he had worked off duty for the same security company, he had not cheated the city for overtime money, yet he had been listed as one of the accused according to Ben's blistering news report. Damn it, DAMN IT. Suddenly, his ringing phone scared him from his deep thoughts.

* * *

"You called my man, you want to meet and talk? I'm down for it, how about your bistro place like before? I want some more of those Rainbow Snaps. Those were good dude and this time I want to try the only other sandwich they had on the menu with actual meat. Does that work?" A surprisingly upbeat Marcus Johnson asked Bens.

"That would be perfect, let's do it again at 7PM, sorry I don't do the cop, military time thing. I always mess it up. I'll see you there tonight at 7, but this time I pay. Well, at least for my stuff, we can go Dutch." With Ben's meeting firmly set, his mind and his gut were far from firm. In fact, both were in a very scary state of flux.

{ CHAPTER 24 }

Bistro time again, the place where plans are made

"So, I see your girlfriend is working the counter again, but isn't that a new, larger hog ring in her nose?" A smirking, close to laughing Marcus asked Ben Morris, as they met at Bathsheba's Rainbow Bistro for a meal and important conversation.

"I don't know if it's new or not, but it is damn big, I never got it, piercings, especially the nose and eye things." Ben replied honestly.

"You sound just like your dad, Mr. Morris, and I never met him in my life!" Marcus chuckled.

"Yeah, well you'd be right on that count, but I want to know what you got from the funeral…oh, wait, I'm sorry to be so blunt. I hope you were able to get through it okay, I know it must have been hard, him being your friend and fellow officer. I'm sorry Marcus."

"No man, you're fine, it was like the funeral of any cop, they suck, but they're predictable. Honestly, I made peace with Kevin in my heart after I heard the news he was gone, so I went at this like a cop would, trying to read a crowd for information at a crime scene; eyes and ears working overtime. As for the ceremony itself, I kept myself isolated in my mind and heart. I couldn't risk allowing either to absorb the reality." Marcus said, continuing, "The thing is Ben, I learned nothing new. It was what I knew before the funeral: cops think he killed himself, the family think he was killed by someone, maybe even by another cop."

"Whoa, whoa, whoa, they think another cop killed him, how does that work?" Ben asked, stunned.

"Shit bro, what are you missing? Damn, it was your big ass story that is setting up the theory and you still don't get it? Okay, I'll lay it out for you in terms that even a non-cop can understand. The security company that those cops, including Kevin worked for, the owner is a straight up cartel funded criminal, a criminal that has deep pockets. Let's imagine for just a minute that some of those, you know, questionably dirty cops, like the ones that might be willing to cheat on Saguaro PD payroll time sheets? Well, they might just be willing to do other things that would get their Boy Scout badges revoked, you follow? I told you already that Kevin Galway didn't cheat the city out of overtime hours, but some of those other officers aren't nearly as clean. I know how they operate, I did my own research, cop research Ben, not reporter research. The rumors are that Kevin was going to dump on the shithead who had hired them, which would put the potentially dirty cops at risk too. Kevin would have agreed to meet with another cop. Both would have likely known of the blind spot in the security cameras. What better place than that to silence Kevin and stop any further investigations dead in their tracks?" Marcus Johnson explained.

"So, do you think that's what happened to Galway then, another cop murdered him and staged it to look like a suicide?"

"Fuck no. First, none of those cops have the balls to do something that big and evil, no way in hell, none of them at least that I'm aware of. Plus, there's no way to explain how they'd have got Kevin's shotgun, shoot him with it under the chin, leave no prints, nothing to indicate any other person was present, that's a tall task. On the other hand, the scene was badly trampled on by responding officers, they destroyed any chance of legit discovery, which is questionable, but then, shock and grief can make people do stupid things. Look Ben, it's been a while now, years in fact, but I've had more than my share of fights on the job and when it's over, you're usually marked up, bleeding even, torn uniforms, shirt tails pulled out from under the belt line at a minimum, these are violent events, not like what you see in movies. Kevin literally had some dirt on the knees of his pants, nothing else that would indicate he was in a fight for his life. "

"So, suicide then is your position and apparently that of most cops, but why? Ben asked.

"Kevin killed himself because of shame and guilt for what we did back in 2001. When those guns were somehow found, I think Kevin saw it as some sort of karmic reminder that we had a debt needing to be paid. I'm not sure I disagree with his take on things."

"That's what you think is the cause, but the other cops, they don't know about that, so what's their reasoning for suicide?" Ben asked, curious as to the possible answer.

"It's hard to say Ben, but deep-down cops all carry secrets. Many silently suffer from PTSD and even their wives, kids, parents, neighbors and friends, they aren't aware that their loved one might be wrestling with demons. Some might actually think Kevin was dirty once the overtime scam was exposed by you. Bottom line is that cops committing suicide is a dirty secret in the trade, so it never really surprises other cops when it happens."

"Christ, Marcus, you don't paint a pretty picture. In fact, it's damn depressing. Speaking of depressing news, what I'm going to tell you isn't what you'll want to hear right now" Ben stated.

"Hey look! Ms. big-chest nose ring is bringing our order, nice! Once we get it and I have some food in my belly, I want you to tell me everything you found out about those guns Ben. Then, over some dessert and coffee, we'll lay out a plan. For now, I'm looking forward to more of those Rainbow Snaps, I'm getting fat coming to this place man, and I'm blaming you all damned day long, son!" Marcus was sincerely looking forward to his food and already suspected that what he was going to hear will only cement his decision about how to move forward. He also knew that Ben wasn't going to like it.

{ CHAPTER 25 }

Channel 14 headquarters, Saguaro

It was just after 10 AM and Channel 14 news division assistant producer Sandy 'Sandman' Kritzer had already been working 6 hours out of his normal 16-hour workday. Longer if a big story broke. The fact was two big stories developed recently, the North-side Serial Rapist and the mysterious death of a recently buried Saguaro PD Police Sergeant. As big as the stories were, without any new information to report, they were becoming stale. Without an arrest, or sadly, another rape, Sandy doubted he would he'd ever get the break needed to drop the 'assistant' from his job title in lieu of full Producer, something he desperately sought to achieve.

Such was his mindset when he received a call from an unknown number. Upon hearing the voice of the caller, he strongly considered hanging up, not needing more crap right now. For some reason, pity he supposed, he remained on the line.

"Sandy, hey man, I know you're busy right now. The noon segment, dinner act and late night are coming up, so I won't hold you, but I've got something you'll be interested in, and, well, I really need a favor." Ben Morris said quickly, trying to get in as much as he could before he was hung up on.

"Yeah, hey Ben, you called it; I'm literally up to my ass in alligators and coyotes, but like I told you before, I can't help you with anything job-wise dude. Your name is not up for discussion, anywhere, that's just the way it is right now." Sandy stated abruptly.

"No, please, Sandman, wait, that's not what this is about. This is something big. I'm sitting on the story of the century, and I need a way to get it out. It's complicated and I can't even give you a proper summary over the phone. I need to meet with you. Believe me, you record this interview and it goes to air, you'll be the lead producer. Not only at Channel 14, but national media will be knocking on your door, it's that big." Ben said, pleading his case.

"Ben no one will give a shit about a reporter who survives drugs and jail to only find a redemption story, it's been done a hundred times, it won't fly." Sandy said flat out.

"Out of control cops, corruption, murder, suicides, illegal guns, Mexican drug cartels. Does any of that sound like the boring redemption story of some lowly reporter who fucked over his own career and found religion, Sandy?" Ben replied, suddenly angry, surprising himself.

After a very long pause, Sandy finally asked, "What the fuck are you into Ben? If this is legit, we need to talk, soon, like tonight soon. When and where?"

"Bathsheba's Rainbow Bistro in the art district downtown, let's do 9PM later tonight, it's where I work now." Receiving confirmation from Sandy, Ben wordlessly hung up the phone.

Just like that, Ben has another date at his workplace, meaning he will need to call and explain it to his boss, Shelley Conner. This would likely cause her to ask more questions than he wanted to field, but in the bigger scheme of things, it was worth the hassle. Ben was making progress, but to what end? He was sure the trip going forward would not be easy.

* * *

Sandy wasn't exactly sure what had just happened. Even if Morris's story could have been substantiated, he wasn't sure how he could air the news without the associated toxicity. He would hear the details first and then decide if he would commit. Sandy wanted to help, yes, but Ben had screwed up badly. In Sandy's opinion though, Ben's treatment by the station and the media community at large, had been baffling. Like a close-knit family, they protect their own. There had been media personalities involved in sex scandals and DUI's, but for the most part, those incidents had been quietly swept under the rug. There had been another case where the son of an influential, competing station owner, had accidentally shot and killed a friend during a hunting trip. Police investigators alleged that all members of the hunting party had been drinking heavily, a potential scandal. After heavy initial media coverage, news of the event quickly faded and was soon forgotten, as if it had never happened. Sandy expected a similar situation when Ben's troubled story came to light, but that didn't happen, not even close.

First things first; hear the story and hope Ben was not simply desperate to find a way back in front of a camera. Worse, what if he was still using drugs? Sandy decided that he would listen to what Ben had to say. He felt he owed him that much, but would not hesitate to draw the line at helping fuel a drug addicts' demise. One thing was for sure, tonight would be interesting.

{ CHAPTER 26 }

A residential home in north Saguaro, Arizona

It had been over two weeks since Saguaro Police Officer Marcus Johnson revealed his plan to a reluctant Ben Morris, who in turn reached out to a friend, Sandy 'Sandman' Kritzer, an assistant producer at local TV Channel 14. More importantly, Sandy had been the only person that would take a call from Ben, as his past was still considered too radioactive for any news organization. However, the breaking news Johnson promised to tell Ben in a taped interview was tantalizing enough that Sandy was more than willing to take a gamble on this potentially career changing move.

The interview location was a nearly 4000 square foot, tri-level home in an affluent part of the city. The home was owned by Sandy's ex-wife Beverley. Sandy knew the house well because he used to own it, but lost it to Beverley as part of the divorce settlement. Divorce aside, they stay on speaking terms and, in an odd way, considered themselves friends. The fact was they both maintained the relationship for situations such as this, when one of them needed something. In this case, Sandy needed a private, secure place to tape a potentially explosive interview. Sandy had even arranged a big night for Beverley to attend a comedy show at a downtown theater, along with a few friends, after tapping a contact in the business for hard-to-get tickets. He expected the interview to conclude and the house vacated hours before Bev would return with her drunken entourage.

It was clear to Sandy that Ben had regained his 'sea legs' as he masterfully guided Marcus Johnson through an incredible narrative, a tale that at first seemed too fantastic to believe, but quickly became all too real and ugly. Marcus's sincerity and the manner in which he delivered an open confession of wrong doings, it seemed impossible not to believe. No doubt about it, this would be gold when released, at least for Sandy and possibly Ben too. Marcus Johnson though? He would probably end up in jail, so why was he doing this? What the hell was his angle?

As they broke down the equipment, Sandy told them it would take at least a couple of days to edit the footage, which he would have to do during his free time, the few hours off for sleep he gets depending on workload. Once done, Sandy would call Ben and from there, they would review it together and come to an agreement as to exactly when Sandy would go to the management of the station with the story. The timing may be further exacerbated with Sandy having to convince the station to participate because the interview involved pariah, Ben Morris. In Sandy's opinion, that will likely be the hardest part to accomplish.

All parties reached an agreement on the rudimentary plan which seemed solid enough. They now had to follow the script. This unlikely band of compatriots exited the house with a new purpose, Ben hitching a ride with Marcus and Sandy riding solo in his BMW. Before they reached their cars in the curving brick driveway, Sandy asked Marcus his burning question, an answer needed before he'd be willing to go forward with this crazy endeavor.

"Marcus, I just met you, I actually believe what you said on camera, but why are you doing this? You realize that once this is released into the wild, it's not going to bring anything but misery for you, maybe even jail? What am I missing?"

"Misery, you mean, for me? I've known nothing but misery for over 20 years now. This is redemption, Sandman. This is the shedding of a burden too heavy to describe. No, my days of misery are over. Live, die, whatever, I've told my story now, I've cleared my conscience. The last 'Horseman' is finally hanging up his spurs. What we agreed to is what's going to happen; I'm so good with it you can't imagine." Marcus answered, finally at peace.

Ben was sick about it. Unlike his vital contact in the industry, Sandy, a media mercenary always looking for the story to advance his career, Ben, somehow, found himself a different sort of person altogether now. He had once been with the 'shark-like' mindset, that of the Sandman, but no longer. Whether it had been the fall from grace, the rehabilitation from drugs, or the time spent in jail, he didn't know for sure, but since meeting Marcus and hearing his story, he felt little confidence that he could again be a force in the media, no matter how powerful the story. In fact, he was no longer sure he even wanted to return to that way of thinking and life.

Ben's reflections upon his past destruction and future hope of redemption, however, pale in comparison to his worry for his new friend Marcus Johnson; nothing good can come out of this situation for Marcus. Oddly enough, with each passing day, as Ben searched for whatever it is he was missing, Marcus was somehow finding exactly the right course of action to pursue. Marcus had admitted to Ben, Sandy and potentially the world that he had actively committed crimes that inadvertently caused people to die.

Instead of feeling disdain and scorn, Ben found himself admiring and trusting him more than any other person. Marcus's honesty, remorsefulness and willingness to admit such things to total strangers, as Ben shamefully admitted to being, he found himself sitting in awe of the man. Ben realized again that this plan was not going to end well, but he had locked in, making sure Officer Johnson's wish for his story to be told, would come to pass. Ben swore to himself, he would do his part, no matter what. He had been assured that Marcus understood the implications.

"God, if you're really there, please help us." Ben found himself, a non-practicing Jew, someone that had never in his memory said a prayer, saying one silently for his friend, Marcus. It was going to be a rough ride for Horsemen and non-horsemen alike.

{ CHAPTER 27 }

Bathsheba's Rainbow Bistro,
morning coffee time

It was close to 9AM. Ben Morris was serving coffee and baked goods from behind the counter, while also delivering the same to the small tables and booths, that were always crowded early in the morning hours, before the brutal Arizona heat had the upper hand. The cook, and right hand to the owner, Shelley Conner, and all around 'shot caller', Jesus was in back baking and doing everything that made a restaurant successful. Ben had been here since 7AM and did not know when Jesus arrived; he might even sleep here as early as he seemed to show up. Ben was happy to finally be working; it gave him spending money, kept his probation officer off his ass, and more importantly, his mind from events that were currently in play.

After the taping session with Marcus Johnson, assisted by the producer, Sandy Kritzer and interviewer, Ben Morris, both leading Marcus through a production that could be aired by any willing media source, hoping for the opportunity to break this fascinating story, Sandy had been editing the footage. As far as Ben was concerned, it was ready for prime time Channel 14 news or held under wraps until the time was right. Sandy might have other ideas based on when to release because he wanted the attention the piece would surely bring, primarily a promotion to full Producer, at Channel 14 or any outlet he chose, if the story breaks the way he anticipated.

That was the way it worked in media. Ben was once held in high esteem as a fierce investigative reporter. Now he was working 'off the books', for minimum pay at a bistro, praying Sandy would find a way to get the taped interview on the air. That would be a tall order considering Ben's past scandal that saw him spend six months in the county jail. Ben was also deeply concerned about his newly made friend, Marcus, and the incriminating interview he had insisted on taping. Once televised, Marcus' career as a police officer would be over and he would likely face criminal charges. Ben had been experiencing tremendous guilt pangs by facilitating the interview, but on the other hand, he held deep fears that if he did not accommodate and assist Marcus in this endeavor, Marcus would take his own life, like that of another recently buried cop that had been involved in this unbelievable saga. Weighing his options, Ben would rather see Marcus alive, facing legal trouble, much more than as a suicide victim. Again, working helped Ben keep his mind off such things.

* * *

Suddenly, the Channel 9 morning news anchor person, Sonia Kee announced loudly: "We're receiving breaking news that there has been some sort of shooting at a mid-city elementary school here in Saguaro…I'm sorry I'm getting this live in my ear, wait, I believe we have field reporter, Maria Flores at the location. Is this correct? Maria, can you hear me? This is Sonia at the studio, Maria are you there?"

The television screen switches to a hectic scene in what appears to be a school parking lot, with sirens screaming and police cars screeching into the location with heavily armed men wearing helmets and vests, shouting at everyone to move away, even field reporter Maria Flores, who was now moving off camera. The scene was one of chaos.

The screen goes back to the Channel 9 studio where the ever

professional, Sonia Kee, was trying to gain control of what was obviously a fluid situation. She assured the audience, saying, "As soon as more information is available, we will be here as the first to report on this breaking story; I will repeat that a shooting at a mid-city elementary school has been reported and a heavy police presence is on scene. We're going to take a break and will return shortly with the latest breaking news by our Channel 9 team who are on the scene, we'll be right back."

This was not good news for Ben and apparently not for the suddenly vocal crowd of generally peaceful, artistic sorts that believed the 60's revolution was more important than 1776, something Ben never offered an opinion on. Amidst loud grumbles about abolishing the NRA, firing the occupant of the White House, and having FOX News shut down, Ben chose to respond only to the plea of raising the volume of the TV for the next news report. Fear started setting into Ben.

After the commercial break, a much more composed Sonia Kee returned. "We're back now, being the first to report news of a breaking story, reported gunshots at a local mid-city elementary school not far from our studios, in fact. I understand we now have new information, from our very own, Maria Flores, who is on site, and has been since shortly after the event took place. Maria, what can you tell us now from your vantage point? Do you have any more information we can report to our viewers?"

Field reporter Maria Flores, only three weeks with the station, almost in a gleeful tone, reported, "Yes Sonia, thank you. The school is in fact an elementary school, Cactus Wren Elementary School, a long-established school that was actually built in the late 1940's. From what we can gather from parents leaving the campus after dropping off their children, they heard loud pops, which they feared to be gunfire because of the plague of school shootings across this nation that have run unabated because stricter gun control laws have not been enacted by honest lawmakers, and it turns out their concerns were correct, the pops heard were in fact gunshots from what we're getting from police and EMT personnel willing to speak to us."

"Sonia, my camera man Rogelio, spotted an EMT he knew from high school and from what we learned, the lone gunman is dead, no children were killed or injured, however it seems a police officer somehow showed up and killed the gunman. At this point, we're not clear as to what exactly transpired, not sure if anyone else has been injured, but based on how the police presence seems to be no longer operating in a tense fashion, I see many officers taking off helmets and vests as they return to their vehicles, at least from our now distanced vantage point, we believe whatever in fact happened inside Cactus Wren Elementary School this morning, the immediate danger is over. I will be standing by for more updates as they become available, we anticipate a police department spokesperson to be on scene very soon for an official update and hopefully an opportunity to ask questions about what exactly happened this morning. For now, this is Maria Flores reporting from just outside the Cactus Wren Elementary School in the middle district of Saguaro, Arizona, back to you Sonia."

"Thank you, Maria, and please update us with whatever information you can gather. Wow, such a volatile situation! For our viewers, this is the dangerous work our brave reporters at Channel 9 put themselves through to bring you the real news whenever news breaks. Now, moving to another very concerning story. In Washington DC, the president and leaders within congress are indicating they're far away from a budget agreement, and…."

Ben's attention left the television news and his thoughts internalized. He wanted to call Marcus, but was suddenly interrupted by his phone ringing. It was Sandy Kritzer.

"Yeah" was all Ben said.

"Have you seen the news?"

"Yes, I'm watching it now."

"Well, if you're thinking about calling Marcus, don't bother. He's dead Ben. He's dead."

⁂ CHAPTER 28 ⁂

Friends and heroes are hard to find, harder to keep

September in Saguaro, Arizona, was still hot, both in temperature, and media attention. A brave, black police officer, without backup, faced down a raving, armed, shooting gunman threatening school children and staff alike, engaged the gunman in battle, both succumbing to gunshot wounds. Every major media and news organization in the nation, including a couple of international outlets, descended upon Saguaro to cover the story of the officer who sacrificed his life protecting innocent children and teachers. He was a local and international hero. The community response was immense, as streets were lined with "We support our Police" banners, trees are adorned with blue ribbons, and billboards suddenly displayed messages of support for law enforcement. This was a startling contrast to the recent social movement clamoring to 'defund the police'.

Fallen hero and police officer Marcus Johnson had changed the narrative across the nation. Stories of grateful parents, their students attending Cactus Wren Elementary School, flooded multiple newscasts, along with recollections from the students whom remembered "Officer M.J." as being very cool, someone they could trust and go to for help. Discussions erupted supporting the need for brave resource officers, like Marcus Johnson, to be placed in every school, regardless of costs. Other demands included metal detectors and automatic closing doors be installed in every school, increased mental health evaluations for persons going through civil disputes or marital/divorce counseling, along with calls for increased, stricter gun laws. These issues were burning up broadcast, cable, radio and newspaper news, while plans were being finalized for a memorial and the burial of hero Marcus Johnson.

Not surprisingly, Johnson's remaining family wanted Marcus to be buried in Atlanta, Georgia, his birthplace, and where they all lived. Leaving no will or any written instructions behind, the family's wishes decided the outcome. Regardless, city leaders of Saguaro, Arizona, still intend to recognize and honor his service and sacrifice. As sincere as the memorial service would be, it would also deflect the negativity the department had faced about the inability to bring to justice, a serial rapist, and would lessen the attention being given to the unsolved death of another Saguaro PD officer, Sergeant Kevin Galway.

Nearly two weeks later, after the innumerable, sad, emotional speeches, and declarations of love from the heart-broken community and police department, the memorial service concluded. The body of Saguaro Police Officer Marcus Johnson was quietly flown from Arizona, to a small family burial plot just outside Atlanta, Georgia. Sadly, this won't be the last time his name will be mentioned.

{ CHAPTER 29 }

Del Vista West building, Saguaro,
late September 2020

Ben Morris was lying on the bed of his miserable and bleakly furnished room in the Del Vista West building. Once a posh hotel and destination of the rich and famous, today it was a sort of 'half-way' house, home to former inmates, recovering drug addicts, mentally challenged individuals, and the indigent and others that the local government deemed worthy of a rent free room. Ben hated residing here, but today was his day off from Bathsheba's Rainbow Bistro. When physically idle, Ben's mental review, a self inflicted torture, followed a familiar, self-pitying routine: failure in his chosen field of journalism, an ex-con on probation, grieving the loss of a recently made friend, fearful his past actions may have caused the death of another person, ashamed to face his lawyer who defended him even when no one else would. It was more than Ben could bear and why he could not wait to return to work. He was also shamed by the job itself; he considered it to be an act of charity from his boss Shelley Conner.

Like clockwork, Ben anticipated the call that came to his phone, a call he had been avoiding for weeks. This time, Ben has decided to take it and move forward, no matter what.

"Yeah Sandy, what's up?" Knowing it would to elicit a harsh response.

A very excited and angry Sandy 'Sandman' Kritzer responded with a blistering barrage of words and emotions, "What's up? What the fuck is up? God damn you Morris, I've been calling non-stop for three fucking weeks and you want to know what's up? How about you telling me what we're supposed to do, that's what the fuck is up you prick! I'd kick your sorry ass if we were talking face to face, FUCK, I can't believe you!"

Giving Sandy Kritzer time to catch his breath, Ben Morris calmly responded, "Sandy, I know I should have taken your call earlier, but I just couldn't do it man, this whole thing has been harder than I ever thought, losing Marcus like we did."

"I get it Ben, but damn man, I thought I might be able to help you know, ever consider that?" Sandy says, in a more calmed voice, but still clearly agitated.

"Yeah, I'm sorry Sandy, but to be honest I haven't been able to think clearly about anything. I should have reached out or at least taken your calls. That wasn't right and I apologize." Ben sincerely admitted. The fact was that Ben had withdrawn completely, from most everything. Not sharing any insight with the people at work as to his emotional pain, even though they had quickly connected him with the fallen hero police officer. The employees proudly shared with customers, that Marcus Johnson loved the fare and employees of "Bathsheba's Rainbow Bistro". One had to admire capitalism.

"No, no, no, I knew this would be hard man. You and Marcus seemed tight. In the short time I got to know him, I liked him, he was real. You know what I mean, not like us? He was legit in what he said and did. I know what he said about what those cops did way back when. It seems fucked up now, but thinking about it, I can maybe see where they believed what they were doing might be right, their motive at least. I'm not making excuses, but still, Marcus's way of telling it had me in his and the other cop's corner, you know?"

"Yes, I do know Sandy. I have felt exactly the same way, and it bothers me because it wasn't right. It got one person killed directly and possibly two others indirectly. I don't think Marcus would have wanted anyone today to think it was right, that's why he was willing to tell us his story. He did it to tell the world it was wrong, and he regretted it ever happened and that he was party to it."

"Yeah, you're right. With Marcus gone, he won't be able to tell that to anyone now. It dies with you and me."

"Not as far as I'm concerned. We put the tape over the air. Marcus tells his story, simple as that." Ben said without hesitation, having thought long and hard about this and the potential push back.

"Are you crazy Ben? He's a fucking real life hero man! You want to tarnish his name now? That's some serious bullshit dude. No way, I'm not going be part of it. No damn way in hell!" Sandy hotly declares.

"Fine, then give me all copies of the recorded interview. I know you've made copies Sandy, don't deny it. Give them all to me and I'll shop the interview myself, even if I've got to reach out to a national outlet, they'd talk to me. You don't need to be a part of it."

"Now just hold the fuck on Morris, you're not going to cut me out, I'm the one sitting on the recording, not you." Sandy, his temper rising, indignantly said.

"In fact, I don't need you at all Mr. Morris. I'll get management to release it once I tell them what it is. No, the more I think about it, I really don't need you at all now that Marcus is gone, so adios!"

"Ah, but you do need me, Sandy. No matter how you put it out, I'm the one conducting the interview, you can't edit that out. Go to air without me and all I do is call a competing station to give them the REAL story of how Marcus and I came together. They'd take that call all day long. Think about how I can shape that engagement, you comfortable with that scenario Sandman?"

After a long uncomfortable pause, Sandy spoke up, "Look Ben, we're not enemies and we shouldn't let our emotions get away from us. Losing Marcus hasn't been easy on anyone and maybe I lost focus on why I was even brought into this thing to begin with. No, if you think we take the interview to air as we all agreed to, I'm in. I just can't bear the thought of his sacrifice being tarnished and that's exactly what's going to happen."

"Thanks Sandy, I mean it. I understand about the emotions of it all, really, I do, it's been hell actually. What we both need to focus on right now is that Marcus came to us for help, and we promised to give it to him. I don't know of any better way to honor his name other than to follow through with our parts of the scripted plan. He did his part; he told us the whole story and allowed it to be recorded. Now it's time for us to do ours."

Ben ended his phone call with Sandy and lay back onto his bed, thinking of the huge hornet's nest about to be stirred and busted wide open.

Lives were about to change, some for the better, many for the worse. The city of Saguaro, Arizona would never be the same. Ben thought that it was long past due.

{ EPILOGUE }

Tampa, Florida, late May 2021:

Ben Morris was looking toward the ocean from the balcony of his second story condo unit, enjoying the warm salty breeze. It was a big change from the dry, hot air he had grown used to in Arizona. Much more had changed for Ben besides the climate. The fact was, Ben's pleasurable balcony experience was a break from his current working assignment: writing a book about Saguaro Police Officer Marcus Johnson, his former police partners, "The Four Horsemen" and their troubling saga.

It had been nearly nine months since Marcus had been laid to rest, with full honors, and posthumously deemed a hero for his actions in stopping a crazed gunman raging within an elementary school, losing his own life in the process. Ben still grieved for his friend, even though their friendship was admittedly short, too short in Ben's opinion, which only made the emotional loss more painful. As bad as that was, Ben also struggled with the knowledge that he himself, had been instrumental in tarnishing the name and memory of Marcus. Thanks to Ben, the character of 'Fallen Hero' Marcus Johnson would forever be questioned. Ben acknowledged responsibility and was slowly becoming comfortable with what he had done, healing as each day of writing passed.

The fact was Ben found solace in writing. He was not really a writer, or at least he wasn't before this ordeal. Now though documenting his own self destruction in the world of investigative reporting, journalism, jail, and the crazy experience of meeting and befriending Marcus, he found catharsis. The money wasn't bad either.

When the first segment of a five-part series of the interview conducted with Marcus Johnson was released on Channel 14 Television News in Saguaro, Arizona, Ben's life had turned upside down, literally overnight. Ben suddenly had job offers from every news outlet in Saguaro, and throughout the state of Arizona, along with lucrative offers from national cable and broadcast networks. Ben had not been alone with offers of new opportunities. His accomplice in getting the interview recorded and televised, Sandy 'Sandman' Kritzer, had doors opened for him like he had never dreamed. He was currently living in New York City, working for the highest rated cable news outlet to date. Ben and Sandy still kept in contact via calls and texts, but Ben had noticed a drop in frequency, fully expecting them to cease before long, which was okay.

It should have been the happiest of times for Ben, but it wasn't. He was still in a state of shock and grief. More than that, he felt he had lost his appetite for investigative journalism altogether. His former boss, Shelley Conner, encouraged him, saying, "Get back in the saddle Pretty Boy, don't be moping around here, you're bringing down business!"

Ben would always be indebted to Shelley and considered her to be a friend; they talked regularly.

Someone else that encouraged Ben to accept an offer from one of the many news outlets was Julio Chavez, his former Hohokam County Probation Officer. Thankfully, Julio Chavez had become very affable and seemingly helpful. The transformation of Chavez's personality had come shortly after Ben agreed to sit down, ironically, with a reporter from Channel 14 News, for an interview about how he had been able to deliver such a hard-hitting piece, that of the Marcus Johnson story. Being a man of his word, Ben had heaped loads of praise upon Julio, regarding his compassionate, ceaseless assistance given to formerly incarcerated individuals as they were pleasantly and successfully assimilated back into society, now as fully engaged and productive members.

At the time, Ben remembered thinking that he felt like he'd just thrown up a bit in his mouth, praising Julio, but he powered through it. It worked. Two months after the interview, Chavez was promoted to lead supervisor overseeing all probationary officers within the Saguaro district, the largest within the county. And before that, he had recommended that Ben be released from probation altogether, which was agreed to by a superior court judge. Julio was currently being touted as a leading candidate in the upcoming fall election cycle to fill an open seat within the Hohokam County Board of Supervisors and would likely win, according to most polling groups.

Still, Ben had not been able to stomach the thought of maneuvering through the petty politics, drama, and back stabbing that existed off-camera within every news outlet he'd ever worked. It simply no longer appealed to him, although he found himself with almost zero money, a soon to be cancelled EBT card, the building superintendent had informed him that he no longer qualified for a room, had three days to vacate and to make sure the room was clean before he left. That had been when Ben received an offer that surprised even him, when he had thought life had no more surprises; to write a book, with options for a movie screen play, royalties of terms negotiable and a firm upfront offer in the six figures payable immediately. Ben had been stunned and had felt completely out of his league. He had negotiated and agreed to several contracts in his working career, but nothing to do with writing a book with the possibility of a movie; it had been simply beyond him. He had known someone he could reach out to thankfully. It was someone he had decided to contact already, not to ask for help, but a person Ben desperately had needed to apologize to.

The place overlooking the beach and ocean, where Ben was writing his book, was also where he lived with his former defense attorney, now quasi-legal advisor, and full-time lover, Ann Warnyk. Ann continued to work as a successful defense lawyer in Tampa, Florida, while also overseeing Ben's contacts with publishers, movie producers and Saguaro, Arizona attorneys. The city attorneys continually threaten Ben with frivolous civil lawsuits, if he intends to continue with the idea of publishing a book of 'unfounded' allegations against a fallen Saguaro police officer.

Ann was a savvy, determined woman. She understood the law and knew that what Ben was doing was legal. More importantly, she loved him. At the same time, she realized, as did Ben, the city's desperation in the matter. Many changes in the ranks had occurred, over the past several months. For instance, a rather young, Randall Jenkins was now the lead Civilian Crime Lab Technician in the Saguaro City Crime Lab. Supervising Sergeant Vernon 'Vern' Kerley, along with his Lieutenant, Larry Osco, had since quietly retired. In fact, several other senior patrol officers, sensing the time was right to leave the force, suspecting an imminent 'top to bottom' inspection coming, they either retired or moved to other agencies.

Closer to Ben's newsroom roots, shortly after Sandy Kritzer left for a national market, a purge of sorts happened within the local Saguaro media community. Owners and senior management second guessed their so called assembled talent; how had they missed the obvious opportunity by not embracing Ben after his release from jail? How had they clearly failed in facilitating his story going to air, and somehow, impossibly, allowing his chance meeting with Marcus Johnson to happen outside their control? Logic doesn't matter in the news industry; ratings, advertising and money rule the day, nothing else.

Ben had found himself immediately as an outside observer and spectator to the Saguaro police department response to the Marcus Johnson story. Oddly enough, he had never been directly contacted by anyone in the department for questioning related to his relationship with Marcus. At first it had been puzzling to Ben, but eventually he had realized they were going to great lengths to not lend any credence to the story. No matter how they had wished and tried for it to go away, reporters from all media across the nation had been asking questions and demanding answers. After several weeks, public pressure had built to a point that a department spokesman, along with the Chief of Police, had provided a prepared statement, immediately followed by a press conference. The strategy the city had chosen was one Ben found to be very interesting to say the least.

As Ben had listened to the prepared statement, it had become immediately clear that the police department and City Hall had no intention of portraying the fallen officers, Marcus Johnson and Frank Garcia, as anything other than that of brave heroes. Although they had found the story told by Marcus to be compelling enough to 'look into', internal investigations had found nothing to conclusively corroborate the details of his widely-viewed and troubling interview. The fact had been, without Marcus alive and able to answer questions and support details, the interview was nothing more than unsubstantiated hearsay. Anticipating a backlash of skepticism and criticism, the police spokesman, followed by the Chief, had provided some interesting details and suppositions as to why Marcus had agreed to the taped interview.

Ben had not been able to pull away from the television screen, holding on every word spoken from the police statement. It had been remarkable the way they had spun it. In the initial statement given by the police spokesman, few details had been offered, but once the chief began speaking and was peppered by questions from the media, the chief had quickly deferred back to the spokesman for a deeper explanation of the investigation. According to the spokesman, the city crime lab had in fact confirmed the fingerprint of a former and deceased Saguaro Police Officer, David Chiang, had been found on the rifle used to shoot and kill Officer Frank Garcia. However, that had been countered with the general knowledge that Chiang's fingerprints could have been introduced while he had been employed as an officer working in the Southern Vista Precinct, where he had legally confiscated many firearms. Unfortunately, many, if not all, of the weapons previously confiscated by Chiang and other officers, had been stolen from an unattended police transport vehicle, temporarily parked within the confines of the precinct, which had been prioritized for storage at the downtown armory. Although the case remained unresolved, confidential sources, had led the department to conclude that those very weapons had been stolen by members of a Mexican Drug Cartel operating heavily at that time in South Saguaro. In the department's opinion, Officer Garcia had found himself in the middle of a criminal, drug shootout, and had taken a bullet, which had then, sadly ended his life.

Slick work Ben had thought. He had wondered how many cops and lawyers it took to think through these answers and bullshit theories. Questions about any tie-in to recently fallen Sergeant Kevin Galway, based on the Marcus Johnson interview, had been dismissed out of hand. Sergeant Kevin Galway's case remained open with absolutely no connection to anything alleged in the Johnson story. To Ben, the obfuscation had been unexpected.

Ben still struggled with whether he had been responsible for Galway's suicide because of the investigative report regarding an overtime scam involving several officers working for the Saguaro Police Department. Galway had been named. That story should be insignificant after all that had happened, and with what he had learned since he met Marcus, but it still bothered him. Ben may never uncover the circumstances behind Galway's death, but at least his wife had received his death benefits from the city.

Since the department decided to portray Marcus Johnson as a fallen hero, not a dirty cop, how had they explained away his interview? Cleverly, they had suggested that Marcus had been suffering from PTSD, which had clouded his thinking. So much so, that with retirement looming, the department speculated that Marcus might have been looking to make money with the idea of a book or movie script, much like a toxic police detective in California who had once worked an infamous case involving a sports legend that had been accused of killing his former wife and friend. That detective's desire for fame and success outside the job had enabled, many believe, a guilty killer to walk free.

That presumption had angered Ben when he had heard it then and it angered him now. This renewed exasperation provided the continual motivation needed to push through the laborious process of writing a book; not easy work, especially for someone who really wasn't a writer by nature. Ben refused to allow Marcus to be disparaged as a mentally confused gold-digger, no matter how wrong it had been in how Marcus had brought it upon himself. That was simply something Ben would not allow to happen. The only way he would be able to defend Marcus and his legacy was through writing Marcus's story for the world to decide; forget the Saguaro Police Department top floor and City Hall.

Whatever way the pendulum of public opinion swung, the story of the 'Four Horsemen' would forever blur the line between 'the good guys and the bad guys', at least for Ben. Others can decide for themselves.

What did he think of his old profession, that of the journalistic media arena? Ben now thought them corrupt, not in terms of money, but deeply lacking in integrity and honesty. If this book becomes successful, he would agree to do interviews, simply out of financial necessity for advertising purposes. Other than that, Ben's career in that industry was over. Agreeing to interviews to further advertise sales of his book, Ben realized his own connection to that corruption and part of him felt disgusted. That alone drove him to focus more on the positive outcome: to honor the wish of Marcus by getting the true story told to as many people as possible.

Breathing in the salt air riding the breeze onto his balcony overlooking the beach, Ben's writing break was officially over. Suddenly, he stopped, overcome with a flood of emotion, realizing that he had managed to escape the snake pit of a sad, petty life. Ben was not just moving forward toward a new future, he was helping a friend. It was perfectly clear; Ben had simply followed the script, and for once, it had finally worked.

About the Author

Stacy Wright is a retired husband, father and grandfather living in Arizona with his wife. Writing for a hobby, primarily to entertain family and friends, he has previously published three story collections, known as the "Blackcloud" books. "Follow the Script" is his first venture into serious fiction.

www.ingramcontent.com/pod-product-compliance
Lightning Source LLC
LaVergne TN
LVHW010109170826
845678LV00012B/2321

* 9 7 9 8 4 6 9 7 6 1 2 7 3 *